Trail of GREED

About the author

John Dysart was born in Fife and graduated from St Andrews University with an MA in Economics and Politics. After qualifying as a Chartered Accountant in Glasgow he pursued a career in Europe working for various international companies. He spent the last fifteen years working as an independent consultant before turning to writing. This is his first novel. He currently lives in France.

Trail *of* GREED

John Dysart

The Choir Press

This book is a work of fiction.
Names, characters, business, places and incidents are products of
the author's imagination or are used fictitiously. Any
resemblance to actual events or locals or persons,
living or dead, is entirely coincidental.

Copyright © 2013 by John Dysart

All rights reserved. No part of this publication may be
reproduced or transmitted in any form or by any means,
electronic or mechanical including photocopying, recording or
any information storage or retrieval system, without prior
permission in writing from the publisher.

The right of John Dysart to be identified as the author
of this work has been asserted by him in
accordance with the Copyright, Designs and
Patents Act 1988.

ISBN 978-1-909300-10-1

Published by
The Choir Press, Gloucester

*To my mother, father and Jud – and anyone else
who recognises bits of themselves.*

Chapter 1

A knock on the door at three o'clock in the afternoon of a fresh Thursday in May.

"Now who the hell could that be?" I thought to myself, slightly annoyed at being disturbed from my reading. I put my book down on the table at the side of my armchair, levered myself reluctantly upright, cursing my bad back, and went to open the door.

I wasn't expecting anybody. I very seldom had callers now – unless it was Mrs. Clark from next door with some delicacy that she had baked that morning.

I could see no one through the smoked glass panel in my front door and wondered, for an instant, if it was some kids playing tricks. The old prank of ringing the doorbells of elderly people living alone and then running off up the street had not yet died out. In a way I was glad. I'd done it myself as a boy and, annoying as it was, I reckoned it was pretty harmless.

I opened the door. If it was somebody trying to sell me something I was ready to send them packing.

"Yes?" I enquired politely as the door swung back.

"Good afternoon, sir. I'm sorry to disturb you, but are you by any chance Mr Robert Bruce?" was the response from a well-dressed man, who looked about my age, standing a few yards back on the path. There was a slightly nervous, enquiring smile on his face.

Neatly dressed in an open-necked shirt and jacket, he had a full head of grey hair, cut short, and a small, slightly bronzed, face lit up by bright brown eyes. About five foot ten, I would guess. He was one of the lucky ones, like me, who had stayed slim with age and didn't have to worry about how to cope with a paunch which prevented him from seeing anything below waist level.

"Yes. What can I do for you?"

The man's face relaxed into a genuine smile and he thrust out his hand to be shaken. I automatically returned the gesture before I realised that such a greeting was not quite habitual in a small Scottish village in the middle of Fife. The unusualness of the encounter was confirmed by his next words.

"Mr Bruce, my name is Pierre Collard. I am French, as you can probably tell from my accent, and I am over here in Scotland for a visit."

I could think of nothing suitable to say except "Welcome to Scotland".

"Thank you." he replied. "Actually I have been here a few times before but, there are a couple of specific reasons for this particular visit."

Being naturally friendly, and having assessed him as an interesting-looking character who seemed to pose no danger, I responded amiably.

"How can I help you?"

"Mr Bruce, this may seem strange to you, but I am staying just down the road at the Fernie Castle Hotel for a few days. I am travelling on my own and would like to invite you to dinner this evening. Perhaps I can explain to you then?"

That rather took me by surprise and I reflected for an instant. A stranger turns up on the doorstep and invites you out to dinner. Not a very usual scenario.

"If you don't mind me asking – why me? Do you often knock on people's doors and invite them out to dinner?"

"To your second question – no." He smiled. "And to

your first question, I have a particular reason – two actually – but I would prefer to explain to you over a good meal. The hotel has an excellent wine list and, as I do know a little bit about you, I thought you might appreciate sharing a bottle of Château Maucaillou with me. Would you be so kind as to accept my invitation?"

"Why not?" I said to myself. He looks like a nice guy and I instinctively accepted. It sounded better than the bridie and peas that I had planned.

"Fine." I told him. "At what time?"

"How about seven thirty?"

"It'll be a pleasure."

He thanked me for accepting and proffered his hand again by way of a goodbye, returned to his car which he had parked ten yards up the road and, with a wave and a "See you tonight", he drove off down the main village street.

I watched the car disappear and went back inside, closing the door thoughtfully. It would make a change. He had looked pleasant and interesting and I genuinely enjoyed meeting new people. There was always something to be learned from anybody, no matter whom. It was a philosophy I had had all my life and I didn't see why I should drop it just because I was "getting on a bit".

My life for the last three years had been a quiet process of adjusting to the solitude of widowhood. That knock on the door was about to change all that and add to it a dimension that I would never have imagined.

After thirty-nine years of a very happy marriage, my wife Liz had passed away suddenly from a totally unexpected stroke. The following six months had been very difficult as I had had to adjust to the immediate loneliness and the prospect of a solitary retirement. Life can deal some pretty nasty blows.

Our son Callum had made his life in Australia and we had had no other children. So I had eventually sold the big house in Stirling and returned to my roots – the Howe of Fife. I now lived in a perfectly comfortable little cottage (minimum upkeep) in the tiny village of Letham and had slid into a calm, but reasonably satisfactory, rhythm of life suitable to a fairly fit sixty-seven year old. I had my books, the garden, my golf course was only five miles away and there were plenty of other great places to play within an hour's drive. I wasn't complaining but I have to admit to a little boredom from time to time.

I tried to return to my biography of Talleyrand but couldn't concentrate. M. Pierre Collard clearly knew who I was and he had announced two reasons for his trip. I had no real connection with France apart from a few camping holidays when Callum had been young and, after he had grown up and gone off to conquer the world, a few golfing weekends in Brittany and Normandy. I spoke a bit of the language but that was all. I pondered over this for a while but soon came to the conclusion that there was no way on earth that I was going to guess what this was all about. I'd have to wait until the evening.

I didn't know then that I was about to make a life-changing discovery and thoughts of fraud, corruption and murder were definitely not on the agenda.

I pottered around in the garden for a couple of hours until it was time to organise myself for my evening out. I was actually rather intrigued by the idea of getting to know M. Collard a bit better and decided that Fernie Castle deserved a relatively smart Bob Bruce. So I dug out a not-worn-very-often pair of smart cotton trousers and ran an iron over a shirt. I slipped on my old blazer and set off in anticipation of an interesting evening.

The Fernie Castle Hotel is only about two miles out of the village and is a comfortably elegant place. Previously home to a wealthy family whose name I couldn't remember, it had been bought by a brewery and turned into a first- class hotel. They had got their strategy right because the central part of Fife (the Howe) doesn't lack money. It is very rich arable land and there are a large number of well-to-do farmers. There are also the country estates of many who had made their piles of money in the second half of the nineteenth century from coal, jute, linoleum and the financial markets of Edinburgh.

M. Collard was waiting for me in the reception area of the hotel. Deep blue carpet on a stone-flagged floor, granite walls and a couple of suits of armour on guard. We greeted each other with another handshake and he suggested we repair to the bar for a pre-dinner drink.

Ensconced at a table in the corner of the dimly lit bar I watched him go up and order the drinks. He was obviously perfectly at ease in his surroundings. The girl behind the bar seemed impressed by the Gallic charm and he came back shortly with a pair of inviting glasses of a nice, deep amber liquid that was not unknown to me.

"Alors, M. Collard, comment allez-vous ce soir?" I asked him, with, what I hoped, was a reasonable imitation of a French accent.

"Verry weel, tank you verree mooch!" he replied with a grin.

We clinked glasses and quietly appreciated the first sip of what he informed me was a fifteen-year-old Glenmore.

He sat back and looked at me for a few seconds, as if trying to weigh me up. I had nothing to worry about so I just left him to it.

He then proceeded to explain to me that he had already been twice to Scotland but had only toured the west and the north – the Highlands and the Islands. This was the first time he had visited Fife and he loved it. Not so rough and barren – more akin to his Normandy. He had been to the charming fishing villages along the coast. He had visited the ancient Palace of Falkland and climbed the hill behind the village. It had been a clear day and he had seen the two Forth bridges in the far distance. From the top of the East Lomond you can see practically all of the county, or Kingdom to give it its proper name. He was planning a trip to St Andrews the next day.

I fully agreed with his comments on the beauty of the area. I had been raised in the village of Falkland and the whole area was home to me. That's why I had moved back here two years ago.

"Robert – may I call you Robert?" he asked, "Shall we go and see what the chef has to offer this evening?"

"Certainly. But if you don't mind, I prefer Bob," I replied. "As you can imagine, with a name like mine, I suffered a lot of teasing when I was young and decided Bob was better."

"OK, Bob, let's go and eat."

I had my father to thank for the Robert. When my mother had questioned his choice, apparently his reply had been "If he gets hassle at school it'll be good for him". It certainly got me into a good few fights in my early years but, with hindsight, I now felt that Dad hadn't got it far wrong.

Once we were seated and had perused the menu we decided that a local fish dish to start with and a good Aberdeen Angus steak would be perfect for both of us. The Château Maucaillou was ordered and once uncorked was put reverently on the side table to be served with our steak.

Still very curious about this unexpected visit and invitation, I broached the subject that I had been pondering over that afternoon.

"So, Pierre, what's the particular reason for this trip and how come you knocked on my door this afternoon?"

"Research into family history," he replied.

"Let me guess. One of your ancestors was an officer in Napoleon's army, like MacDonald?"

"No. Not so far back as that. In fact my father was Scottish."

"With a name like Collard?"

"No. That's my mother's name."

He saw I was intrigued and he then went on to explain.

"There are quite a few of us in France of our generation who were brought up not knowing who their fathers were. It's not surprising when you think about it. At the end of the war there were thousands of British, American and Canadian soldiers, young and away from home, and French girls are quite attractive. Many of the girls married and went back home with their soldier husbands. Some didn't. My mother was one that didn't and I was born and brought up not knowing who my father was – although I had a rough idea."

The fish arrived and we both seized our utensils and got stuck in. I was intrigued, being a bit of a history buff.

"Go on," I said.

"Well, to cut a long story short, I am sixty-nine years old. I was born in 1944. I wasn't the only boy in the village not to have a father. Some had been killed, some had gone home. When I was old enough to ask, my mother explained to me that my father had 'gone away'. It was only later, when I was about ten, that I wanted to know more. She then told me that my father had been a young Scottish officer. He had been dropped into occupied France to liaise with the Resistance in preparation for the

Normandy Landings. My mother was also in the Resistance and they had become firm friends. I suppose it is practically impossible for us to imagine the stress that these young men and women were under. It was only after he left that my mother discovered that she was pregnant. I was born and she raised me on her own. She never married and she kept a photograph of him beside her bed until she died about fifteen years ago."

Pierre finished off his fish and sat back with a satisfied look on his face – a handsome firm-featured face, slightly tanned. His brown eyes turned on me as if hoping that I was interested.

I was. "So you've decided to trace back your roots?"

"That's about it," he replied.

"How far have you got? Is there any way I can help?"

He reached into his inside jacket pocket and pulled out his wallet. He carefully extracted two photographs, lent forward and placed them on the table in front of me.

Chapter 2

I set down my wine glass and picked them up. They were slightly faded and crinkled at the edges and he had clearly kept them in his wallet for years.

One was a formal studio photograph of a young soldier in officer's uniform; the other had been taken outside and was of the same man, not in uniform this time, standing beside an attractive brunette, his arm around her shoulders. They were both smiling at the camera.

"This is your father and that's your mother?"

He nodded.

"And you said that you've come over here to find out what happened to him?"

He nodded again.

"But, in fact, you do know what became of him," I said.

"I know now – but I only discovered about a year ago. I had obviously wondered all my life and when I retired I decided to try to track him down."

I sat back in my chair and looked at him closely. He said nothing but was watching me attentively.

"Is this some kind of a joke?" I shot at him.

"Absolutely not. These two photographs sat on my mother's bedside table for about forty years. As I said, she only discovered she was pregnant after he had had to leave to go back to Britain. She hadn't expected to hear from him again because she knew he had a fiancée back in Scotland. They had both known that their relationship would be temporary. There was a war on and at that time nobody knew how it was going to turn out. Bearing in mind that they lived constantly under the threat of arrest, or worse, they lived out their romance knowing that it would be short lived. He never knew of my existence."

I managed to register most of what he was saying whilst my mind was racing in all sorts of directions.

"My mother absolutely forbade me to attempt to find out what had happened to him. As she said, he might well have been killed. Better to remember what we had, she used to say. However, after she died and I retired, curiosity got the better of me and brought me over here."

My consternation was slowly subsiding. I picked up my glass and took a large mouthful of that delicious wine and let it roll around in my mouth before swallowing it gently. I put the glass back down and looked at him again. Still that same half-nervous, half-questioning expression on his face.

I held up the photograph of the smiling couple.

"I've never seen this photo in my life, but this one," holding up the studio portrait, "has hung on the wall of my mother's bedroom all my life."

"And ...?"

Although I had had a shock I somehow adjusted to it rather quickly. I suppose it was because I rather liked this guy.

I looked across at him. He was clearly nervous about my reaction. I shook my head slowly from side to side and allowed my mouth to form a half-smile.

"The randy old bugger!" I said, slowly, pausing gently on each word.

This man's father was the same man that I knew as my father. It sounded incredible but there was the evidence in front of me. There was no way he could otherwise have had a copy of the photo I knew so well. My sister and brother also had copies.

I had to believe Pierre's story. It rang true. And, as Pierre had said, I'll bet Dad wasn't the only one.

It was perfectly understandable that such circumstances could have happened. I knew Dad had spent a year in France but knew no details. We kids had assumed that it must have been very dangerous. Whether his relationship with Pierre's mother had been love or simply an intense friendship between two people living on the edge I would never know but, knowing Dad, I figured that I understood how it could have happened. He had come back to my mother and they had had a very happy marriage so I felt no need to criticise him. He had never known about the pregnancy, how could he?

I noticed that the wine bottle was almost empty.

"So, as it seems that I've just discovered I've got an older half-brother – and he's paying for the dinner – I reckon you'd better order another bottle."

Pierre's face relaxed into a contented smile. He clearly had hoped that I would not be too shocked by the news and he made appropriate signs to the waiter who appeared shortly with another of the same.

Conversation after that was naturally a little slow as we both adjusted to the fact that the news was out. I would occasionally stop in mid-sentence and shake my head in surprise.

We both were intensely curious to explore each other's experiences of the last sixty-odd years. He was clearly desperate to know about his father but didn't push too hard while I took my time to get used to the idea. I was fascinated to learn about his upbringing in Normandy and what he had done with his life and conversation started to flow more and more smoothly in direct correlation to the diminishing level of the wine in the bottle.

The manager eventually threw us out – or politely asked us to vacate the restaurant – at about half-past eleven. By then I was in no fit state to drive so he kindly offered to drive me home. Pierre and I parted at the door, agreeing that we should give ourselves a day to get used to our new relationship.

Just before parting company one of my habitual off-piste thoughts came into my mind.

"Pierre, you don't by any chance play golf, do you?"

"Where did that question come from? Yes, actually, I do."

"Good or average?"

"I used to play to eleven or twelve, but that was a good few years ago."

I smiled. "Right. It must be Dad's genes. Day after tomorrow I'll take you to my club. It's very near here and he was a member there for as long as I can remember."

Pierre said he'd be more than happy and I was levered into the car to be escorted home.

Next morning I awoke rather late. Although it was May, the night had been very cold and there was still rime on the grass at ten o'clock. But the sky was clear and the air was fresh, which was more than could be said for my head. I was getting past it, I said to myself. A whisky before dinner, a full bottle of Bordeaux and a couple of brandies after. There was a day when I would have taken that in my stride. Not now.

The state of my head reminded me of the discoveries of the previous evening. I decided to go for a brisk walk up to the post office to get some milk, in the hope that the exercise would bring me more or less back to normal. Why did Mrs McLachlan's voice sound twice as loud as usual? I made it back home and headed off into the kitchen to make myself a cup of strong coffee.

I walked past Dad's photograph on the wall. It was a larger, framed version of the one that Pierre carried around in his wallet. I stopped and looked at it with an affectionate smile. I'd walked past that photograph hundreds of times but from now on it was going to be with an added piece of knowledge.

"Well, Dad, how are you this morning?" I asked him. "I've just found out something about you!"

The expression on his face didn't change – if it had I would have thought I was in Harry Potter country – but the eyes looked out at me, smiling. His silence about that year in France now took on another meaning. We had assumed that his reticence had to do with the horrors he'd seen or the friends he'd lost. I knew now that there had been another reason. What a pity we had not been able to talk about it. Perhaps if Mum had gone before him he might have let it out but that hadn't been the case. She had survived him by four years and he would never have talked about something like that while she was still alive.

Next problem. How do I tell Mike and Heather? I had asked Pierre if he was aware that he had acquired, apart from me, another younger brother and a sister. He had known, he had told me, and I suggested he leave it to me and I would organise the breaking of the news to them. The question was "What was the best way to do that?"

Heather was eighteen months younger than me and we had been close playmates as children. We had, however, gone to different schools and different universities so our paths had separated. We remained good long-distance friends, seeing each other two or three times a year. Her world was very different from mine but we kept in touch. She had married a farmer and lived in the centre of the country outside Doune, where she had dedicated her life to her two kids and a never-ending collection of horses. She had always been keen on horses and had studied veterinary science at Edinburgh. It was through her work that she had met Oliver and that had settled her life for her. I wasn't sure what her reaction would be.

Mike was a very different kettle of fish. Mike had come along six years after Heather, so he was my junior by seven and a half years, a difference which had meant that we had shared very little when we were young. When I was discovering the fair sex he was still playing with his Lego.

But we had both inherited the combativity and competitiveness of our father, expressed through different outlets. I confess to have done reasonably well at my rugby and cricket and had found that I could turn my hand to most sports. Mike also had that gift but took up pursuits that I had not – squash, hockey, biking and the like. The only area where we had a real common interest – and that developed later – was on the golf course.

Mike had gone into the army. He had discovered that if he joined up as a student he could earn a salary whilst studying. The only commitment he had had to make was to stay in the service for seven years after graduating. This didn't bother him at all and he had stayed on after his seven years and carved out a satisfactory career for himself. He had been able to retire in his fifties with a perfectly adequate pension.

He had seen the world, with service in the various trouble spots across the disappearing British Empire, until he was, much to his regret, superseded by a younger generation. During the last fifteen years of his service he developed his administrative talents in a series of logistics postings. He had never married and now lived in Forfar, in striking distance of the Cairngorms, with Oscar, his black Labrador, where they could both continue to keep fit by wandering off into the mountains for a few days whenever he felt like it.

He was inordinately proud of his dog, claiming to have trained him to sniff out drugs at twenty metres, and he maintained that he could find his way home on his own from anywhere within fifty miles away. I hadn't believed this piece of boasting and, a couple of years ago, Mike had proposed a bet (a green fee at Gleneagles) that he would prove it. We had driven forty miles up into the mountains and he had simply stopped out in the wilds, let Oscar out of the car and we had driven off back home. He had turned up two days later for breakfast. And on top of that Mike had beaten me three and two over the King's course the next Tuesday.

I decided I would tell Mike first about his new brother and then we would both discuss breaking the news to Heather and Oliver.

I phoned Forfar and got him at home.

"Hi, Mike, how's life?" I asked.

His cool, laid-back voice came back down the wire.

"Fine, but unfortunately a bit quiet. I've been planning a hike but I'm going to have to delay it because the forecast is looking a bit dodgy."

"Good," I replied. "Fancy a bite to eat this evening? We haven't seen each other in a while and I have to be over in Dundee this afternoon. Why don't you drive down and I'll buy you supper?"

We arranged a time and place to meet and I spent the rest of the afternoon going over all that Pierre had told me – trying to adjust to the concept of the newly-enlarged family.

Everything he had said had rung true and I found I liked him. I had absolutely no reason to doubt his story but, on the other hand, I had no way of checking any of it.

Dad was dead and he had kept nothing from his time in France. Also, if it was all made up, what possible reason could Pierre have of inventing such a tale? It's not as if there was an estate to claim or any potential material advantage that could come his way. Could there be some other motive? Then I remembered that he had said that there were two reasons for the dinner invitation. What could the second one be?

Chapter 3

Mike arrived at the small Italian restaurant just five minutes after me. I was already seated at the table which I had reserved in advance. He breezed in, causing a few female heads to turn as he made his way over to me.

Although still a bachelor, and liking it that way, he had never had any trouble in attracting the opposite sex. He was not a big man but he had presence. His graying hair was kept short, military fashion, his features were clean cut, his skin tanned from his outdoor life and he projected an aura of total self-confidence, without any hint of egoism. I'm here, I enjoy life, take me as I am or leave it, it doesn't bother me.

Not long after he had bought his current house and decided to settle down I had paid him a visit. I had been amused to discover that, in his living room, he had a collection of fifteen or twenty framed pictures on the walls and on the bookcases of attractive women of various ages and seemingly different nationalities.

"All your conquests?" I had asked him.

"Not all," he had replied with a grin.

"A bit strange to put them all on display," I said.

"It sort of happened by accident," he replied and then proceeded to explain.

"In fact the whole idea started as a bit of joke years ago. I had a couple of pictures then and I once forgot to hide them when I invited someone back for the night. On that particular occasion the girl stayed for about a week and then left to go back to Australia. A week later

I got a parcel through the post with that photograph over there inside it".

He pointed to the photo of a fun-looking brunette smiling at the camera, perched on the roots of a palm tree on what looked like a tropical beach.

I strolled over and picked it up for a closer look. As I was putting it back I noticed the message scrawled in blue ink on the back "For your collection! – X".

"So I decided to leave them out permanently and the collection has just 'kinda grown' – like Topsy," he said with a grin. "I suppose I must attract the type of girl that doesn't have any permanent designs on me so they think it's rather fun and when they send me photos 'for my collection' I stick them up!"

I didn't mind his collection at all, but I did know that Heather was rather disapproving of it.

"Well, how's tricks?" he asked, as he sat down, "and what world-shattering event has induced you to put your hand in your pocket to buy your wee brother a meal? It's you that's paying, isn't it?"

"Oh, nothing much. I'll tell you after we've ordered – and, yes, I'll pay this time."

We dispensed with the logistics of ordering lasagne and a bottle of wine, and after a bit of small talk – Seen Heather recently? – How's Oscar? – I decided to plunge in, but not without dipping my foot in the water first to judge the temperature.

"Mike, did Dad ever talk to you much about the time he was in France during the war? He never discussed it much with me but, you being in the army, I wondered if he spoke to you about any of his experiences."

"Nope – hardly a word. All I know is that he was some kind of a liaison officer with the Resistance and it was a question of living on your nerves non-stop for months. I think he lost a few friends and I just assumed he didn't want to drag up old, bad memories."

Or perhaps old good memories, I thought to myself.

We had, all three, been very fond of Dad – perhaps the relationship with the boys had been closer because we had had more common ground – sport especially – and he had been an only child and hadn't been quite so comfortable with girls. I was hoping that Mike's reaction to the news I was about to tell him would be much the same as mine. I suspected it would.

"Why?" He looked at me thoughtfully, put down his fork and took a sip of his wine. "That's something we've never talked about before – so what's the reason now? Has something cropped up to do with that?"

"Not something, but someone."

He looked intrigued.

"Someone who was out there with him? Whoever it is he must be in his nineties by now. Go on."

"Well, yesterday I had a visitor – a Frenchman – who said he was over here on holiday and he invited me out to dinner at Fernie Castle. He seemed a pleasant enough guy so I accepted."

"Very nice too. But how did you manage? You don't speak much French."

"Oh, that was OK. He speaks perfectly good English. And shut up for a minute. Don't interrupt while I tell you what happened."

As I explained the whole story to him Mike's face went through a series of expressions which would have done justice to a chameleon.

When I had finished he looked at me thoughtfully.

"And you believe him?"

"Yes, I do. He seemed perfectly genuine. His story's perfectly plausible. But the real clincher was the photograph.

It's a smaller version of the same photo that hung on the wall in the parents' bedroom all these years – the one which we now all have a copy of. How else could he have that photo if not from his mother?"

"And the other photo. What did the girl look like?"

"Brunette, good looking. A bit in the style of Mum actually."

Mike sat back and rubbed the top his head with his hand.

"Wow! The old bugger never told us about this."

"He wouldn't, would he? He came back to Mum, got married and here we are – all three of us. This man – Pierre Collard is his name – insisted that his mother never found out that she was pregnant until Dad had gone back home and, as she had known he was engaged, she never told him. She probably wouldn't have known how to contact him anyway. I don't know about you but I can easily imagine how it happened. If she was in the Resistance and Dad was undercover liaising with them life must have been bloody dangerous. I suppose in circumstances like that you would, let's say, 'forge mutually comforting relationships'. You certainly would, that's for sure!"

Mike didn't comment.

"I'll bet there are hundreds of similar cases. And probably most of the kids born like that were simply told that their fathers had been killed. Easier for everyone."

Mike sat back, thinking it through. He took another sip of his wine and put the glass gently down on the table. He looked across at me with a grin.

"So what do we do now?" asked Mike. "I suppose we'll have to tell Heather."

"First of all, you've got to meet him. He plays golf – maybe it's Dad's genes. Anyway I invited him for eighteen holes at Ladybank tomorrow. I thought you might come along and hack your way round the course with us. Gives you an opportunity to meet him and, if your feelings are the same as mine, we'd better cart him over to meet Heather and Oliver."

Mike was obviously still absorbing the news and only half-listening. He was slowly shaking his head from side to side then a wide smile spread across his features.

"The randy sod," he said, – but there was a genuine tone of affection in the way he said it, "But then, I suppose ..." His voice trailed off.

"What was that you said? Golf tomorrow? OK, what time?"

"Eleven. I haven't told Pierre that I would bring you so it'll be a surprise for him. It'll be interesting to see his reaction and you'll get an opportunity to come to your own conclusion about whether he's telling the truth or not."

It would also give me the chance to really see what kind of a man Pierre was. It's difficult to judge the true personality of someone over a couple of bottles of good solid red wine but on a golf course it's a different matter.

The way a person reacts to success or adversity is a good pointer to their character. And there is a lot of that in a round of golf. How he reacts on losing a hole, or winning a hole, on missing a three-footer on the last green or on driving two balls in a row into the deep rough are all very good indicators of personality.

We caught up on each other's news for the rest of the meal – my attempts at gardening, Mike's recent hike in Skye with Oscar – finished off with a coffee and I settled the bill. We made our farewells on the pavement outside the restaurant. Mike promised to be down by nine thirty the next morning and we'd go over to the course together.

I had arranged to pick up Pierre from the hotel. Mike and I arrived just before ten. I left him in the car and went into the reception to find Pierre. He was waiting in the bar reading the newspaper when I walked in. We greeted each other as recently acquainted friends would.

A "Good morning" and "How was your headache yesterday morning?".

"I decided that I needed some fresh air yesterday," he grinned, "So I went off to St Andrews for the day. I also thought I'd better get myself some clubs because I haven't brought mine with me."

"You needn't have bothered. You could have hired some at the club for the day."

"It's not a problem," he replied. "I've been meaning to get some new ones for a while."

I then told Pierre that I had a surprise for him. He looked at me curiously.

"I've invited your other half-brother to come and play as well. I thought it was a good opportunity for you to meet him."

I'm sure that he paused for a split second as he was getting up from his chair but he covered it up with a slight stumbling movement, as if he had caught his thigh on the table. A slight look of concern crossed his face – as if he would rather that I hadn't – but the moment passed very quickly and his composure returned. It had only been for the briefest of moments but it did make me think that perhaps I should have discussed it with him beforehand.

"You don't mind, do you?"

"Not at all," he said. "I was hoping I would get to meet the others while I was here."

We walked out to the car, and as we approached it the door opened and Mike climbed out.

He came towards us with a smile and held out his hand

to greet Pierre. What could have been a slightly awkward moment passed off very smoothly.

"Delighted to meet you, Pierre. Bob has told me the whole story – or as much as he knows. I must admit it was a bit of a shock at first but I've kind of got used to the idea now. I had always thought I only had one older brother so it's a bit strange to discover that I am now only third in line for the title."

"In line for the title? What title?"

"Oh there is no title. It's just an expression. And, even if there was, there would have been no castle or estate that went with it. Come on. Let's go and play some golf."

Pierre went over to his car, opened up the boot and proceeded to haul out a brand new golf bag filled with a complete set of Mizuno clubs, a box containing a pair of shoes and a shiny caddy. Mike and looked at each other.

"Blimey, that must have cost you a packet," I said.

Pierre grinned. "I felt like treating myself."

We stowed his gear in my car and set off for what every golfer hopes will be an enjoyable eighteen holes, where every drive goes down the middle of the fairway, where all the putts drop and at least one green side bunker shot ends up in the hole. But it never works out that way!

Conversation was a little difficult as Mike was in front and Pierre in the back of the car so I filled in the time on the short fifteen-minute drive by explaining a bit of the history of the course he was going to play. How, back in the 1870s, the locals of the village had invited Old Tom Morris, one of the father figures of golf, to come over from St Andrews and help to design a short golf course for them. He had cycled the fifteen miles and, in an afternoon, laid out a course of six holes then cycled back home again with his twenty five pounds fee in his back pocket. Later they had added three more holes to make it into a good testing nine-hole golf course where, as a boy, I had learned the rudiments of the game.

Since then it had been extended to eighteen holes and it was now recognized as one of the most testing courses in the county and, whenever the British Open was played at St Andrews, it was used as one of the qualifying courses.

We were lucky as the weather was reasonably clement. Clear blue sky, no sign of rain and hardly any wind. As it was mid-week there were few people on the course and it looked like we would be able to take our time. I had no idea how good a golfer Pierre was but I did know Mike's game. I think the best adjective to describe it is "flamboyant". There tends to be a great deal of effort put into his swing but not so much technique. I had given up years ago giving him advice. It just pissed him off. The only time I gave him advice now was if, by the fourteenth, it looked like he had a chance of beating me. That was the moment to make little suggestions to him about how to improve his swing.

It was good harmless fun. Mike was happy if he managed a couple of blistering drives, a few long puts and a par or two. These would then form the major part of the conversation in the bar afterwards. He just liked being out in the open air where he could exercise his love – hate relationship with the little white ball.

My approach was different. I did like to work at the game and apply as much intelligence and course management as my old body was capable of. Golf is entirely up to you. You can blame nobody but yourself if you don't play well. It doesn't matter what the conditions are, the challenge is to adapt to them and to play to the best of your ability. That's what makes the game great, as far as I'm concerned.

Nowadays the old bones and muscles are not as they

used to be and I have had to accept that I can't hit the ball so far. But age and experience have improved my short game which means that I am actually still scoring as well as I used to – even if not quite at the level of Tiger Woods. I still console myself with the thought that, if I do chip in from twenty yards, I know that Tiger couldn't have done any better.

We unpacked our gear, shoed up and strolled over to the first tee.

"How many strokes do I get?" asked Pierre with a grin.

"None."

"Wait a minute. That's not reasonable. I haven't played for several months; I don't know the course and I've never played with these new clubs before – and on top of that, over here you guys drive on the left!"

Mike and I looked at each other.

"I suppose he is our guest," I said. "Tell you what. We'll toss a coin. If you call it right you can have one shot on each nine to use when you want, but you must announce it on the tee before you start the hole. OK ?"

He called heads, won the toss and off we went.

Pierre, we discovered fairly quickly, knew how to hit a golf ball. Being physically fairly small and wiry, his swing was compact and he relied on timing for distance. No great heaves of the club, just a smooth swing, a nice wrist movement and the ball flew effortlessly off the face of the club. After a few holes he started to get the hang of his new clubs and he and I settled down to a tight contest. He was three down by the eighth but had caught up his deficit by the time we got to the fourteenth. From then on it was stroke for stroke for the next four holes.

All square on the eighteenth tee.

Pierre and Mike had got to know each other during the round and seemed to be getting along fine. I had intentionally left them walking up the fairways together as much as possible. I wanted Mike's impressions of him to be as little influenced by me as possible. That little hesitation when I had announced that he was joining us still made me wonder a bit. When we had shared our dinner and the wine had been flowing I had perhaps not been as alert as I should have been. Once I had got over the surprise of his story I have to admit I wanted to believe him as I had instinctively liked him. There was still the second reason why he had wanted to meet me and that hadn't come out yet.

We still had the eighteenth to play. It's actually not a difficult hole when you know it. Seeing it for the first time, however, it looks rather daunting. As you stand on the tee with the flag in the distance waving in front of the clubhouse you're starting to think of that nice cold beer. But between you and that beer there is a drive across an immense dip in the ground which stretches completely across the course in front of you and is all rough. To reach the fairway there is a carry of about a hundred and fifty yards but it looks more. If you don't make it you're dead. It is full of hillocks and patches of heather and the only clear ground is the path that wends its way through this mess of vegetation.

Pierre looked at it with apprehension. I wasn't going to tell him the distance. It looks further than it really is. I grinned at him.

"All square and one to play?"

"Sure – no problem."

It was my honour. On a good day I could clear it with a four iron but that would be giving away the fact that it was not as long as it looked. So I took out my three wood and fortunately hit a clean one straight up the middle. You can't see it bounce on the other side but I knew I was fine.

Pierre was up next.

"I don't suppose you're going to tell me the distance to the fairway?"

Mike and I exchanged glances. Two smiles and two shakes of the head.

He had seen the club I had taken. He knew that I hit the ball just a little bit longer than he did. What he didn't know, and I did, was that I had landed probably fifty yards clear of the rubbish in front of us.

He teed up his ball, hesitated a bit over his choice of club and finally plumped for the driver.

We could feel the tension and the nervousness as he started his back swing. Unfortunately for him he forced his shot. The hands came through just a bit too quickly and, although he hit the ball cleanly with the centre of the club face, the result was a solidly hit slice. We all watched the ball curve gracefully through the air and finish up amongst the trees on the right of the fairway.

"Bad luck."

Mike and I were both very sympathetic but he realised that he had been had.

"You bastards," he said, "That ball's miles over."

"But not straight I'm afraid," said Mike with a grin.

"You wait. The hole's not finished."

We wended our way down the path and up the other side in a solid spirit of comradeship. It had been an enjoyable game and Mike seemed to be getting on well with his newly acquired half-brother.

We finished the last hole in good spirits. A par for me. Pierre hit a lovely four iron out of the trees and chipped on to about four yards. Mike managed to chip in from twenty yards short of the green which made his day. We conceded Pierre's putt, explaining that it was a tradition of the club to do so to someone who was playing the course for the first time. I don't think he believed us but accepted it gratefully.

After stowing away our clubs in the car and changing our shoes we repaired to the bar to refresh ourselves and ease my aching muscles.

"Pints all round?" asked Mike, still looking disturbingly fresh and chirpy.

He brought them over to us at a table by the window, sat down and grinned at us. He was still basking in the glory of that twenty-yard chip on the eighteenth. All the thrashing around in the rough earlier was completely forgotten.

Pierre and I exchanged a resigned glance as he relived his moment of glory. It had been an enjoyable round and amply served its purpose. I had seen Pierre on a golf course and it had helped me confirm my initial impressions of him.

"Well, I suppose we'll have to organise for you to meet your half-sister now. I haven't asked you how long you're planning to stay in Scotland."

Pierre didn't answer at once. He seemed to be trying to decide to say something but wasn't sure if it was the right moment. After a pause he addressed himself to me.

"Do you remember that I told you that there were two reasons for my trip over?"

"Yes."

"Well I'd like to tell you both the second reason. I need some advice, or some help, on a financial matter here in Scotland."

This came as a bit of a surprise. What kind of financial matter could Pierre be involved in over here?

Naturally I said I would help him if I could, little imagining the dramatic consequences that we were all about to get involved in.

Chapter 4

A quiet beer in the bar of the club house is, I suppose, as good a place as any to be the starting point of a major change in the direction of my life. Especially at the age of sixty-six.

When I look back on it I wonder what Liz would have said if I had come home to her with the news of an unknown brother and the prospect of a much more active retirement than I had envisaged. She'd have taken it in her stride, I think. She had always been very pragmatic about my sense of adventure and my sometimes cock-eyed ideas. Much as we had had a wonderful relationship, since my retirement she had had to adjust to me being around the house much more than before and upsetting the rhythm of her life. She'd probably have welcomed anything that took me out and about.

"So how can I help, Pierre?"

"Let me get us all another drink first," he said and went over to the bar to order.

Mike looked across at me, "What do you think this is all about?"

"I haven't a clue, but we'll soon find out."

Pierre came back and carefully deposited the drinks on the table and sat down again.

"The other night over dinner I told you about how my father happens to be the same man you both know as your father. I was distinctly nervous as to the reaction I would get as you can probably well imagine and, if you remember, most of what we talked about was him and how it had all happened."

"I didn't tell you much about myself. I first of all needed to know how you would react and how we might get on with each other. The fact that we are sitting here together after a very pleasant morning, enjoying a beer, leads me to believe that you've both got over the shock and that we will be good friends. I certainly hope so. I'll never be able to have the closeness with you two that you have with each other, having been brought up together within a family situation, but I hope we can get somewhere near it."

He paused for a moment, perhaps waiting for a confirmation, or at least some kind of reaction.

Mike jumped in.

"Pierre, I didn't have the pleasure of the dinner and the wine but Bob has told me the story. He's convinced."

"And you?"

"Don't take this the wrong way. You're a nice guy. You tell me that you're my half-brother. I would like to believe you. I enjoy your company. Give me just a little more time to get used to the idea. We've only just met."

"Fair enough. I can understand that. As far as I am concerned that's enough for me to explain the second reason for me being here."

He then proceeded to give us a quick sketch of his life – his upbringing in a village in Normandy, his schooling and his further education. He briefly told us about how he had lost his wife very soon after they were married and about his decision to throw himself into the business he had started up.

It turned out that he had been in the right place at the right time. He had, with a few friends, started up an IT company in the mid-seventies and it had been enormously successful. He had become a workaholic. All that had mattered in his life had been his company. His only real outside pursuit had been golf. To cut a long story short his original associates had one by one left the company and he had found himself as the last of the original shareholders, sitting on a lot of money. He didn't tell us how much.

"A couple of years ago I realised that perhaps it was time to stop. My health was still good but I was getting on a bit. Why not enjoy the rest of my life?"

He was watching us closely as he developed his story.

"So I sold the company and found myself, at the age of sixty-seven, with plenty of money and lots of free time on my hands. I travelled a bit for a few months and then started to think about what I was going to do. Meanwhile I had to do something with the money. I bought myself a couple of houses and invested the rest. Most of it was with banks in Switzerland, but I wanted to spread it around a bit and, because of my Scottish connection and the Scots reputation for careful investing, I thought I would put some into an Edinburgh asset management firm. I looked around and found a medium-sized outfit called Ailsa Investment Management and came over to meet them. They sounded as if they knew what they were doing.

"It's a company that only deals with individuals and not with company money. They have a few funds, ranked by risk, and their market is the elderly individual who wants their money to be reasonably safe. The kind of people who want to hand something down to their children or grandchildren when they go but, in the meantime want to generate a reasonable revenue to add to their pension or pay for their old folk's home or whatever.

"It sounded like it made sense to me so I invested some money with them in their medium-risk fund."

He paused for a moment or two and took a sup of his beer.

Mike and I exchanged glances.

Pierre put his pint down carefully on the table, pulled out a handkerchief and carefully wiped his lips. He continued.

"This is where I have a problem," he said. "I put my money in about two years ago. Since then, as I guess you know, Bob, the markets have been doing reasonably well. I looked at the returns of various similar funds around Europe and they are all performing at around six to eight per cent per annum. AIM has averaged three and a half."

"So we Scots are not so hot after all?" I suggested.

"I don't know. I just don't like the smell. Their quarterly reports are all very bullish and positive but the performance doesn't match up. I tried to get details of where they had invested but just got complicated marketing speak that I couldn't make head or tail of. I don't have any financial expertise. Anyway, while I was doing all this digging into Dad's background and managed to find out about you guys' existence, I discovered that you had a financial background. So I wondered if I could ask you for some help or advice."

Naturally I replied that I would be quite happy to do what I could to assist.

"In what way do you think I can help?" I asked.

"I'm not quite sure yet. I have a feeling that the guy that runs this outfit is, let's say, not totally above board. It doesn't seem logical to underperform like that. But maybe there's more to it."

"What do you mean?"

"Well, he steers clear of the corporate money – perhaps so that he doesn't have professionals to deal with. He specifically targets elderly individuals. Most of them are probably not very money conscious. Perhaps half of them are already in retirement homes or starting to suffer from dementia. It would be relatively easy to bamboozle them with science."

"You mean that perhaps his fund is performing perfectly well and he is skimming off a chunk for himself?"

"Exactly. When you think about it, the medium-risk fund is worth fifty million pounds. Let's say he is actually getting a return of six or seven per cent and is only admitting to three and a half per cent – which is a figure that probably would satisfy most of his investors – then the difference of, say, three and a half per cent is a tidy sum. In fact it's one and three-quarter millions."

"Shit!" said Mike, waking up to what Pierre was explaining.

I could see the scenario. And it wouldn't be the first financial scam. Man's ingenuity to mount schemes to fleece innocent investors goes back centuries.

If the company was run by a crook who had no morals or was just outright greedy, Pierre could be right. Most of these people relied on "professional" advice and if the company was smooth and convincing it could work. I didn't know how much regulation there was in the industry but I suspected there would be ways round whatever rules existed. And if you had bent accountants who, for a higher than usual fee, would sign off the accounts you could make a pile of money. Also, if anyone didn't like the rate of return they were getting they would simply cash in and invest elsewhere.

"Pierre, how much did you invest with these guys?"

I shouldn't have been supping my beer when he replied because I gulped and it went down the wrong way.

"Four million."

"Christ!" was the next contribution from Mike.

"And, let's say, three and a half per cent of four million is ..."

"A hundred and forty thousand pounds. But it's not the money. I've got so much I don't know what to do with it.

I could easily just take it away and invest it elsewhere. It's the principle. I don't like being screwed and, if he is doing the same to a bunch of people who really need their money looked after, then I want to expose him. I've got the time to spend and not much else to do."

I've always been disgusted by the thought that there are people who are prepared to stoop to this kind of clearly criminal behaviour. If it was true I could only agree a hundred per cent with Pierre's reaction. I had railed about the financial services industry often enough – like most of the population of the country – but to be, perhaps, close to an actual case put things in a different light.

"If what you say is true, then I fully agree that something should be done about it. I don't have a lot to do either and it could be quite fun."

"Quite fun" is an expression I wish I hadn't used. It was going to be more than that.

We all chewed this over for a minute or two. Mike got up to renew the drinks. I looked at Pierre with a grin, already trying to imagine how we could go about finding out if his suspicions were true or not.

"So what do you have in mind?"

"Well, you're practically local to Edinburgh. I wondered if you might have some contacts. Also with your financial expertise perhaps you can think of a way of finding out if they are up to anything or not. The reason I came over now is that there is a conference in Edinburgh next week on private investment and the AIM boss – a man called Alan Purdy – is to be the main speaker. I'm going to it to hear what he has to say and I wondered if you might come along too."

By this time Mike had come back and set the drinks down with a grin.

"I rather like the idea of this," he said "I know bugger all about finance and money but if these guys are crooks I'm all for bringing it out. Mind you, I don't know what I can bring to the party."

At that point I didn't either but he was going to turn out to be exceedingly useful.

I reflected for a minute or two. I relayed the information to Mike about the conference next week.

"Does this Purdy character know you're going to the conference?" I asked Pierre.

"Yes. I replied to the invitation I received. I suppose they need to know for numbers who is going to attend. I'll probably get a badge at the entrance. That's the way these things usually work."

"Here's what I suggest. You haven't made any waves with these people yet?"

"No. I'm just one of their investors and I get their regular bulletins. I haven't asked any questions about returns or anything like that."

"OK . I'll see if I can get an invitation for myself. We'll go along independently. You stay perfectly friendly with your Mr Purdy and I'll go along as if I was representing potential investors and see if I can stir things up a bit."

"You mean bushwhack him?" asked Mike.

"Something like that. I'll ask a few questions and see if I can destabilise the guy. Pierre stays friendly, on the inside. Afterwards we compare notes. If things look suspicious we'll plan what to do next. I'll tap a few contacts and see if I can get an invitation. How about that?"

"And if we conclude that everything is above board, I'll just decide whether to leave my money there or move it," Pierre concluded.

That decided, I asked Pierre what he was planning to do over the next few days.

"A bit of touring," he replied. "Maybe I'll take my new

clubs with me and get in a bit of practice so that next time we play I can give a better account of myself."

Mike suggested that perhaps we should introduce Pierre to his younger sister. I had forgotten about that but obviously it had to be done.

I dropped Pierre off back at his hotel and Mike and me went back to Letham, having promised to join Pierre for dinner.

We spent the rest of the afternoon at home doing a bit of gardening. Mike is still fit enough to help me with some of the heavy stuff and I have to admit that I appreciated his help. Bad backs are not ideal for shifting heavy sacks of compost or for clambering around in trees to prune them.

Dinner was an opportunity for us to fill in lots of stories about Dad which Pierre really appreciated. It must be strange to discover who your father is at seventy years old. I couldn't help thinking about all these years that we had had when we had taken him for granted and to realise that here was someone who would only learn secondhand. We did our best to regale him with anecdotes which we hoped would give him a picture of the man we had both loved and who had been an integral part of the forming of our personalities. He had been an example to us in so many ways that were incalculable.

The great thing about him had been the example he gave us and also the fact that he had let us get on with our lives – make our own mistakes – but was always there if we wanted an opinion or advice – and most of it was delivered with sound common sense.

Pierre let us ramble on. It was also an opportunity for Mike and me to reminisce. I discovered things about Dad through Mike that I hadn't known about. We each had our own personal experiences that we hadn't always had the occasion to share. So Mike and I benefitted from the memories as well as Pierre. It was a very satisfying evening, and, as usual, the food and wine were excellent.

We parted company rather late and I risked the fact that there would be no police on the two-mile journey home. If there had been I would probably have been in line for a few points on my licence, but the alternative of being driven home by Mike was not an option. He would have turned the balloon into all the colours of the rainbow. I was going to have to put him up for the night and let him go off home the next day. And on top of that he insisted on a night cap before crashing out at around two in the morning.

On Monday I was going to have to see about getting an invitation for the conference and phoning my wee sister to tell her that we had somebody we wanted her to meet. I had no idea what her reaction was going to be but I thought it best to keep it as a surprise rather than announcing the news over the phone. We had decided that we would organise a visit to Doune after Pierre got back.

Chapter 5

Sundays are not very different from any other day of the week when you're retired. Mike woke late and set off for Forfar early in the afternoon.

I did the little housekeeping that I was now used to. A quick vacuum, change the bed sheets, stick on a wash. I have a cleaning lady once a week who does the rest and always leaves the pictures hanging not quite straight. I think she knocks them all slightly off the horizontal just before she leaves to give the impression that she has dusted them. I manage to keep the place in a reasonable state of cleanliness although Liz would probably be horrified.

The last few days had certainly been a change in routine for me and had set me thinking a lot about Dad. I looked differently at the various mementoes of him that were scattered around the house. His portrait on the wall. Other photos and keepsakes that I had inherited. I pulled out the drawer in the old desk and rifled through piles of old black and white photos which represented a pictorial essay of my childhood. Definitely a day of memories – almost all good ones.

I drifted through the afternoon and went to bed early after watching my DVD of *The Man who Shot Liberty Valance* for the umpteenth time.

Fresh on Monday morning I turned my mind to Pierre's suspicions of AIM and Mr Alan Purdy. I still had contacts in the financial world of Edinburgh so, after breakfast, I got on the phone. I had no trouble in fixing up an invitation to the conference on "Investing For You" which was to be held in a Conference Centre on Wednesday.

I was rather looking forward to my outing. The idea of asking a few questions designed to disturb appealed to me. Perhaps shaking the tree a bit might reveal something about the company and its boss.

I don't exactly know why I had suggested that Pierre and I go separately. As I was planning to play the role of the awkward one I just figured that it might be better to have someone more or less on the inside. That way, between us, we might learn more. It seemed to make sense at the time.

Once that was fixed and I had planned when I would have to leave on Wednesday I had the rest of the day to myself.

As we had agreed, I phoned Heather to invite ourselves round at the weekend.

"Hi, Heather, how's things?"

She recognized my voice immediately.

"Bloody awful if you really want to know. One of the horses has gone lame and I'm looking after Rory and Paddy for a few days as their parents have decided to clear off for a holiday in Spain. I'm seriously thinking of charging them for childminding services."

I knew this was rubbish because she adored her two grandchildren but I let her get her frustration off her chest.

"How about you? It's ages since we've seen you. What have you been up to?"

"Not much. The gee-gees."

"You're not in to horses are you?"

"No, my gee-gees are golf and gardening. Listen, I had supper last night with Mike and we thought we might invite ourselves over to see you at the weekend if you're up to it."

"Hold on a minute and I'll check."

Heather's calendar was usually pretty full but she came back to the phone with the news that Saturday was free if we wanted to come over for lunch. I confirmed and we then nattered for five minutes about the usual things – the weather, the horses, Oliver's new car and the bloody government.

"By the way, there will be three of us, if that's ok."

"Who's the third?" she asked promptly.

"Secret. Wait and see."

"Mmmm – male or female?"

She was continually hoping that Mike would settle down with someone but I figured that was a forlorn hope.

"No comment."

We left it at that and I hung up, agreeing that we would be there around noon on Saturday.

Having sorted that one out I thought I would take advantage of the clement weather and go over to Ladybank for a bit of practice. After all, Pierre was away trying out his new clubs and I was damned if I was going to let him beat me when he came back. I also needed to do some thinking about how I would approach question time at the conference.

Thoughts were careering around in my head in random order and I needed to get them straightened out. I've found that there are two ways to resolve this kind of a problem, both based on the principle of externalisation – either talk to someone or write them down. Automatically this process forces you to arrange them in some kind of logical order. Having nobody around to talk to and being too lazy to start writing there was only one other alternative – go off and do something completely different and come back to them later.

I decided to go over to the golf course and hit a few

buckets of balls. I had recently bought a new driver and it needed getting used to.

Twenty minutes later I was standing on the practice ground with two buckets of balls at my feet and a seven iron in my hands.

A couple of loose swings to warm up the old muscles. Thwack!

Reasonably straight, reasonably long, no pulled muscles.

I then settled down to my habitual practice procedure. I took all the clubs out of the bag and lent them against the bench behind me and proceeded to warm up for ten minutes or so with a couple of shots with two or three of the short irons, taking plenty of time between each shot. There's not a lot of point in hurrying. After all out on the course you only hit the ball on average once every two or three minutes. Banging off ten eight irons in less than a minute seems to me to be overdoing it. And who hits two shots, one after the other, with the same club (apart from the putter) – or perhaps the driver if you've put the first one out of bounds?

My theory is that you should allow yourself no more than five or six shots with one club, then move on to the next one. I then finish up with the last twenty balls or so as I would probably play a round – perhaps one shot with a four iron, then a seven, followed by a half shot with a wedge.

Thwack! About a hundred and forty yards straight down the middle. That'll do. Take a different club. Close the face a bit and punch it and watch it keep nice and low, below the wind.

All thoughts of asset management have now evaporated completely. All I see is my little white friend sitting there waiting to be hit, or soaring up into the air designing a perfect curve to fall and bounce on as close as possible to where I intended.

I stop for a few minutes while my imaginary partner is searching in the rough for his wayward drive.

Our green keeper had set up a couple of old rugby poles at a distance of about a hundred and fifty yards and twenty yards apart – that being a reasonable average for the width of a green. At my level of golf nowadays I always aim for the centre of the green. If the hole is near the middle so much the better. If it's towards one side – too bad. It just means I have a longer putt.

So I line up for the middle of the two poles. That allows me a deviation of ten yards either way to still hit the green. I once calculated that this gives me a margin of error of about plus or minus four degrees off centre if I want to land on the green at that distance. I wish I hadn't done the calculation because it scares the hell out of me now whenever I line up my shot!

I finish up by going through the bag until I've hit three in a row with each club within the bounds of the two poles. Total concentration. Grip, feet, alignment – then empty the brain up in my head of all thoughts that might pollute the other brain – the one down in the gut that knows exactly what to do because he's done it thousands of times before. I stubbornly try to hit the ball the way I used to thirty years ago. The technique is still there but the body is a lot less flexible and I have to adjust to that. It's still a great game!

I wearily stack all my clubs back in the bag, lug it over to the car and wander in to the club house for a well-earned beer. Sitting in the bay window overlooking the eighteenth green, watching a ladies foursome earnestly putting out as if the British Open was at stake, I rerun the video of the questions I might ask at the conference and the possible responses. My video could not have imagined the events that were to follow.

I did however have one idea which might be useful.

I had a fairly good friend from the past who might be able to help me. We had been regular visitors to each other's houses when Liz had been alive but when one of the couple is gone there is a tendency to lose touch. George and Helen had, if my memory was correct, a son, Steven, whom we had watched grow up and who had, after university, gone into financial journalism. He was a few years younger than Callum and the last I had heard was that he was working in Edinburgh. It would be interesting to know if he knew anything about AIM.

I got up to leave just as a slightly boisterous foursome came in for their nineteenth hole. I knew two of them quite well, especially the shorter dark-haired, pugnacious looking individual in the plus-fours.

"Morning Keith," I said in passing. "Morning John. Had a good game?"

"Hallo, Bob. Not leaving are you? Stop a minute and have a drink."

Keith and John were fellow members of the club with whom I had occasionally played in competitions. They were good enough characters. Keith, or as I should properly refer to as Sir Keith McDowell, was an extremely successful businessman who had taken over his father's wholesale grocery business and built it up to become the largest chain of supermarkets in Scotland. He had recently been knighted for his success. Short and sturdy, with close cropped dark hair, going grey, he was a vigorous bundle of energy – the kind of man who never walked quietly into a room but bustled in, automatically turning heads. I didn't know him that well but quite enjoyed his company. He played punchy golf, not much style but extremely competitive, and had a fund of rather dodgy jokes.

John Harris was a good friend who ran a veterinary clinic in the nearby town. Being in the heart of farming country and there being little competition, he had also been very successful in his career. Liz and I had got to know him years ago when we had had a dog and the friendship had developed from there.

The other two were unknown to me but were introduced by Keith as Gavin Reid, his lawyer from Edinburgh, and Peter Gibson. No further identification was volunteered for him.

I agreed to a very quick beer, not wanting to be unsociable. We chatted for a few minutes about our chances in the upcoming Ryder Cup. Peter seemed a harmless enough chap, a bit nondescript. He didn't have much to say because, as usual, Keith monopolised most of the conversation. The lawyer from Edinburgh didn't volunteer much. He kept himself rather reserved, in a lawyer's observation mode. He was a bit overweight and balding. A rather supercilious air about him. His weak chin and round, slightly bloodshot eyes said to me that he probably drank a bit too much. My guess seemed to be confirmed when he ordered a refill – large gin and tonic – before I had even drunk half of my beer.

When I had finished my drink I left them to it, promising to give Keith a call soon to fix up eighteen holes.

"This time I'll beat you," he said with his usual competitiveness – half smile, half deadly serious.

"We'll see", I replied and bade them all goodbye.

After a simple late lunch I got on the phone to George who sounded glad to hear from me and asked all the right questions about how I was surviving on my own. He confirmed that Steven was still in Edinburgh and seemed to be doing rather well. There was talk of a permanent girlfriend and Helen was starting to think about grandchildren. He gave me Steven's office number and his home number and said he was sure he would be happy to hear from me.

I tried the office number but he was unfortunately unavailable so I thought I'd leave it until the evening.

I got through to him just after seven and he sounded both pleased and surprised. I gave him an update on Callum whom he asked after.

I then explained, in very vague terms, the reason for my call.

"Steven, you're now working as a financial journalist if I understand correctly from your father?"

"Yep. And I'm quite enjoying it, although a lot of it is much less glamorous than it sounds. Ploughing through Annual Reports, interviewing boring old farts who are only interested in making money – but it pays the rent."

"Can you help me on something? Do you know anything about Ailsa Investment Management?

"Do you mean AIM, the outfit run by a guy called Alan Purdy?"

"Yes."

"Why do you want to know? Thinking of investing?"

"Oh, no. It's for a friend of mine who asked me about them. I had never heard of them but I told him I would try to find out."

"I don't know much but I'll ask around for you. Is it urgent? I do know they are giving a conference the day after tomorrow at the Caledonia Conference Centre. I'm going along."

"Good, so am I. It's at eleven isn't it? Why don't I meet you beforehand and we'll have a coffee. It would be good to catch up."

He was up for that so we fixed a time and a place and I hung up.

Chapter 6

I set off early on Wednesday morning to drive through to Edinburgh for my coffee date with Steven. I had decided that he could be a useful ally if it turned out that there was anything fishy about AIM and I was going to get him onside.

The drive down through Fife was, as always, nice and easy – easy from a traffic point of view and easy on the eye. Skirting round the east side of the Lomond Hills I drove down on the new fast road towards the Forth Road Bridge.

I have always loved the approach to North Queensferry. As a boy there had been no road bridge and we had had to make the crossing by ferry – a great adventure for a young boy.

But the old railway bridge had always been there – a magnificent monument to Victorian engineering skills. It is as much a symbol of Scotland as the Eiffel Tower is of Paris.

What makes it stand out so dramatically is the fact that it's not spoilt by a town or city at either end. It spans the Forth about ten miles east of Edinburgh and stands in superb isolation above the grey waters of the Firth of Forth.

It was the first steel structure in Britain and was opened in 1890. It required sixty-five thousand tons of steel and God knows how many rivets.

Long may it stand.

Steven was waiting for me at the agreed rendezvous. After exchanging welcomes and catching up on his career progress, I told him about my "friend" who had invested some money and wasn't too happy about the performance and wondered if there was anything dodgy going on. I explained how I had agreed to go along and be a bit provocative and see what the reaction was.

"Listen, I'm going to try to upset him. We think there's something behind the non-performance. When we go along you don't know me. We'll go in separately, but we can meet up afterwards during the farewell coffee or whatever. If there is anything fishy going on and Purdy gets uptight by my questions, and then sees me talking to a financial journalist, then he's not going to be a very happy man. If you want to write an article on what you've seen or heard that's ok with me but we do it as if you and I have no prior connection. Keep my name out of it. Tomorrow we can speak by phone and compare impressions. Then we can decide on next steps. OK ?"

Steven listened attentively. I stressed that I didn't want him writing about our suspicions yet. If he reported the meeting straightforwardly, that was fine, but he wasn't to start publically surmising yet. If we thought things were not right and we started digging he would be kept informed and we could decide together whether to go public or not, and when.

"Fine by me. Maybe I'll get a good story out of it."

Little did he know that he was going to get several stories out of it.

As I entered the foyer of the vast glass building, a monument to modern architecture, having laboriously ascended the twenty-five granite steps leading up to the enormous revolving doors, I was asked two or three times if I needed any help. Was I perhaps lost? Was I sure I was in the right building?

I guess that jeans and brown leather loafers, topped off with a bright canary yellow, open-necked shirt, and covered with a light brown canvas jacket were not customary in this environment but I didn't give a damn. I wanted the attention. I was past the age of needing to conform and I was determined to enjoy myself.

I walked up to the reception desk manned (or womanned?) by three bright young things, all smiles and lipstick, short skirts and plunging necklines, who dutifully gave me my badge and my welcome pack – a neat little canvas bag with logos plastered all over it containing the programme and a few advertising leaflets – and I was permitted to pass through into the auditorium.

I had procured an invitation through one of the few remaining contacts that I had in the Edinburgh financial world, so my badge carried my name but no company identification.

The auditorium was about a quarter full which gave me plenty of scope to choose a seat in a suitably strategic position. I chose one toward the middle, about five rows back from the front, right in front of the table behind which the various presenters would be sitting. I was pretty sure I would be noticed.

The auditorium gradually started to fill up as people straggled in, mainly in groups of two or three but with the occasional person on their own. It was a typical cross section of an audience for such an event – a couple of dozen elderly grey – or white-haired gentlemen in suits, shirts and ties – the old school, all around my age – a few little old ladies clearly there to keep an eye on what was happening to their savings, then the next generation: mostly male, most in their twenties, all texting furiously on their iPhones or consulting their iPads and ignoring everyone around them. I think if you asked them afterwards what the colour of the seats was or roughly how many people were there, they wouldn't have a clue.

Perhaps thirty per cent of the younger generation was female – power-dressed in black or grey business trouser suits, sporting large "designer" handbags, (what is a "designer" handbag? I would have thought that every single handbag in existence had been "designed" by someone!), tossing their hair to the side to be able to slide the mobile phone against their ear. Heads tilted, earnest conversations taking place. The occasional wave to someone who passed. It gave the definite impression that it was all for show. Why not go out into the corridor to phone?

Two of the younger males sat down next to me – not so much as a "good morning" – and I received a full whiff of scented gel, mixed with the strong musky perfume of the girl in front. Fortunately on my other side I had a couple of guys of my generation who voiced the standard greetings and we exchanged a few normal comments about the weather, the traffic and last week's rugby match. At least it was human contact.

At the appointed hour the three conference presenters mounted the four short steps at the side of the stage and took their places behind the table, each behind their own name plate. If they had got it right Mr Alan Purdy was sitting in the middle. I looked at him with interest. This was the man I had come to see. This was the guy that Pierre suspected was ripping him off.

He was about six feet tall and I guessed his age at around fifty-two or fifty-three. His face was starting to round out, the cheek bones no longer prominent and the beginnings of a jowl around his chin. The eyes under the slightly bushy eyebrows were blue and gave off the impression of a certain degree of intelligence. This impression was strengthened by a large forehead. He was smartly dressed in a three-piece suit, a blue and white striped shirt and a bright emerald green tie. A matching handkerchief had been thrust casually into his top pocket.

He was overweight – not yet dramatically, but on the way. But it was the mouth that bothered me. Set above a weak, slightly receding chin, his mouth was narrow, held in place by soft thickish lips. The overall first impression was of physical strength and relative good looks – a combination that, if not imbued by humility, tends to develop a liking for power. But that was only a first impression. I hoped that during the conference he would show more of the kind of man he was.

The master of ceremonies walked on to the stage, microphone in hand, beaming at everyone and proceeded to announce the beginning of the conference. Everyone quietened down. The younger crowd dutifully switched off their telephones; the older contingent folded away their newspapers.

This was probably the culmination of a couple of months of earnest work by the man with the microphone and he was basking in the attention. I won't describe him because he didn't really have very much to him that made him stand out. He was just one of these guys that do this sort of thing and as far as I was concerned he could have his moment of glory.

He told us how delighted he was with such a large attendance for the fourth annual conference on "Investing for You" (with a nice commission for him, I thought to myself), and proceeded to introduce the speakers. Each name was greeted with polite applause, a little bit more for Mr Alan Purdy, Chairman and Managing Director of Ailsa Investment Management, but not from me. I'm sparing with my applause – certainly when no one has done or said anything yet. Why should you applaud someone just for turning up? If what the speaker has to say is worth it, I'll willingly applaud – at the end.

There were to be three presenters who would each speak for about half an hour and there would be twenty minutes of question time after each presentation, announced the MC. Mr Purdy, who was clearly the star of the show, would be speaking last – after a coffee break.

I was not in the least bit interested in the presentations on "Succession Planning" or "Tax-effective Investing". I would let them drift by. Mr Purdy's presentation was entitled "Winning with the Big Boys", sub-titled "How the man in the street can gain as much as the large corporate investors". Why he couldn't have thought up a title which was self-explanatory and didn't need a sub-title to explain what it meant I don't know. Probably there was some deep marketing philosophy behind the idea.

The elder contingent listened with attention to the discussion on Succession Planning, which was not surprising. The question session lasted about fifteen minutes and various people could be seen taking notes. After all, if they could pass on as much of their wealth to their children and grandchildren without the taxman grabbing half of it, why not?

Needless to say, each discourse had been accompanied by a bloody Power Point presentation. The "Succession" man treated us to a plethora of family trees with arrows flying all over the place. There was even one which simulated a situation of two men who had formed a civil partnership and adopted two kids, one of which had produced two grandchildren!

The taxman's contribution was a series of slides containing reams of words and numbers and percentages.

He proceeded to read them to us, presumably on the basis that he thought we couldn't read them ourselves.

In spite of the fact that he had announced that we would all receive a hard copy afterwards, the younger generation earnestly scribbled away on notepads. He overran his time by about ten minutes, but that didn't really matter because there were only two questions at the end – both of which were unnecessary because the answers had already been given in the presentation.

We had a short break for coffee in the lobby. I knew nobody, apart from Pierre and Steven, so I stayed off on the side, observing the sheep networking. After a couple of minutes a lady nervously approached me and held out her hand.

"Good morning," she said somewhat nervously. "Are you enjoying the conference?"

I smiled down at her. She looked about ten years older than me, in her mid-seventies perhaps and was wearing a powder blue suit, the jacket over a white blouse adorned with a pearl necklace. Nothing to indicate poverty or wealth. Just a nice person. Her hair was white and neatly kept. She was sporting a black patent leather handbag, clutching a brown foolscap envelope under her hand bag arm and trying not to spill the coffee in her other hand.

"Here, let me help you."

I took the cup from her, placed it on the table beside us and turned back to answer her question.

"To be honest, the first two presentations bored me rigid. I really just came to hear what Mr Purdy has to say."

"Me too. I'm Alice Hetherington, by the way. I don't know anybody else here so I hope you don't mind me importuning you."

"Not at all. My name is Bob Bruce."

"Originally Robert, I suppose," she said with a smile.

"How did you guess? What brings you here?"

"Well ..." she said hesitatingly, and looked intently at me. "I'm also very interested in what Mr Purdy has to say. You see, I'm a client of his and I've given over most of the money my late husband left me to AIM for them to manage. I'm not very good at financial things but I'm a bit concerned about what they are doing with it."

My antennae moved into gear.

"Go on," I said.

"Well I don't know if I should. You look like a nice, trustworthy person – certainly different from all the others here – but I don't know you."

"Mrs Hetherington – may I call you Alice? I'm basically here for the same reason as you. Not for myself, but for a friend who expressed exactly the same concerns to me. I promised him I'd come along here and listen to what they have to say and see if I could help him."

"Are you, or were you, a financial person?"

"To a degree. Let's say I know more than my friend."

"And certainly more than me," she went on.

"The trouble is that I live up in Perthshire and I'm not exactly surrounded by smart financial management people. Our family lawyer knows a fair bit about conveyancing but that's about it."

"Where do you live?"

"Just outside Waterloo."

I knew the village which was just off the main road north to Pitlochry. I'd passed it many a time on trips north and always wondered how it got its name. It must be a village that was no older than the battle but I had often wondered who had named it and why? Perhaps the local squire had fought with Wellington and when he came back he renamed the farm cottages after the famous victory and it subsequently developed into a village. It wasn't exactly the kind of place where you would find a lot of financial expertise.

"What do you mean when you say you're concerned about what they're doing with your money?"

"Well it's not an awful lot, but it's all I've got and I need the income to supplement my pension. It's just not paying me as much as they said it would when I signed up."

"And you're thinking of moving it?"

"I can't yet because it's tied up for five years and I've another three years to go."

People were starting to move back into the auditorium.

"Let's go and see what they have to say and we'll talk a little afterwards, if you're not dashing off."

"No, I'm not. See you afterwards then," and she bustled off inside.

I took my place, ready for the AIM presentation or what I guessed would be the Alan Purdy show. I would definitely have to have a word with Alice afterwards.

Once everyone had settled down Mr Purdy was announced as one of Edinburgh's success stories. He stood beaming and welcomed us all, thanked the two previous speakers for their erudite performances, cracked a couple of jokes which, although not particularly funny, were met by the obligatory laughter – mainly from the younger bunch.

His presentation was slick. There is no doubt about that. Power Point slides with multi-coloured graphs succeeded one another at just the right speed. You had time to absorb the effect of the slide while he pointed out the one or two numbers he wanted you to notice and then on to the next one. There was no way the slide was up long enough for anyone to fully absorb the detail.

The whole thing was very upbeat. Intelligently, he mentioned a couple of investments that had not turned out quite as well as expected but they had not had a major effect on the overall picture.

"We pride ourselves at AIM in our capacity and nerve to take risk – measured risks. That's where the money is. Perhaps not today but at some point in the future we are sure that the risk ventures will come through."

He was in command. He had his audience's full attention. It was a mixture of plain language interspersed with just enough technical terms and buzzwords to sound very convincing. The trouble was it was mostly flannel. He succeeded in convincing everybody that last year's growth of three point nine per cent and the upside potential of the riskier investments, linked to the likely overall economic indicators for the next few years was an excellent performance – even better than the previous year's three point five per cent.

A very satisfied Mr Purdy sat down to applause from the audience and congratulatory handshakes from his fellow presenters.

The Master of Ceremonies then announced that Mr Purdy would be happy to take questions from the hall. As always on these occasions there was silence for a few moments. Then an earnest young lady from the middle of the young bunch stood up and asked the first question. It was something to do with the ratio of fixed and variable returns in the portfolio which could have been answered with two or three simple figures, but somehow Purdy managed to spin out his answer to last about five minutes. Definitely a man who liked the sound of his own voice. He'd have been a good game show host.

Another couple of inane questions followed which were summarily dealt with and then our organiser looked at his watch and announced.

"We've time for one more question."

I got to my feet, a couple of sheets of paper in my hand with some numbers on them which I had jotted down the day before.

I noticed Pierre, Steven and Alice all turn their heads towards me.

"I have a question for Mr Purdy."

Purdy was at this point smiling at the taxman sitting next to him, obviously thinking that his job was done. He wasn't paying much attention to me.

"I'd first like to congratulate Mr Purdy on his very polished delivery."

That got his attention. He smiled at me and nodded his thanks.

I pretended I was consulting my notes and glanced up and eyeballed him. The smile faded slightly. He started to look a little nervous.

"I've been looking at the results of other funds of similar size and the average growth figures I have is seven point two per cent for last year – some hitting as high as ten per cent. I also noted that the year before their average was six point nine per cent. According to my calculations that is a differential of, let's say, three and a half per cent each year, which, for a fund of fifty million, makes three and a half million pounds over the two years. Can Mr Purdy explain to us where this missing money has gone?"

There was dead silence. You could have heard a budgie burp.

The younger generation looked shocked. The older generation woke up.

The MC jumped in.

"Sir, I think your question is out of order."

"I'm sorry," I replied. "Perhaps I didn't frame the question correctly. What I meant was that if investors had put their money in other funds they would be three and a half million pounds better off."

Meanwhile Purdy had rallied from the shock and recovered. He stood up and signaled to the MC that it was ok.

"Mr . . .?"

"Bruce," I replied.

"Thank you for rephrasing your question. You must admit that the way you put it the first time could have led to misunderstandings."

I smiled at him.

"Let me explain."

He started by trying to cast doubt as to whether my numbers were correct and then veered back to the rubbish he had trotted out during his presentation. He gathered steam and managed to steer people's thoughts away from the question I had asked.

When he sat down the MC quickly wrapped things up so that there would be no chance of any more questions from the floor, thanked everyone for coming and invited us all to take a drink outside before taking our leave.

A few of the old guard smiled at me and patted my arm as they passed on the way out.

Most of the audience accepted the offer of a drink and were milling about, slowly congregating into groups. I preferred to stand off on the side by the window and observe. The largest group was near the bar where Purdy was holding court. A few of the young brigade were gathered round him, hanging onto his every word. I also noticed with interest that Keith's lawyer, whom I had met the other day at the golf course, was there too, frowning and making the occasional comment into Purdy's ear. He must work for AIM as well, I thought to myself.

Steven approached me diffidently and made a show of introducing himself, handing me a business card.

"That was a nasty one."

"It was meant to be!"

"Do you mind if I write about it?"

"No, but keep it factual – as we agreed. Don't go wild ... yet. He didn't like my question at all, but he was pretty good at covering it up. I think something is going on. I'll tell you about it in a couple of days – ok?"

"Fine."

I could see that Purdy had noticed us chatting. He wasn't going to come and speak to me in this public environment, that was for sure. But I did expect some kind of reaction to the potential embarrassment I had caused him.

I saw Alice hovering nearby so I excused myself from Steven and welcomed her with a smile as she came forward.

"You seemed to have rather set the cat among the pigeons," she said.

"Well, that was the idea."

"Bob," we were on Christian name terms now. "Do you think it would be possible that you could phone me sometime?" She slipped a small piece of paper into my hand, "So that you could advise me on what I should do about my investments? And, in the meantime, can I give you this?"

She handed me a large brown envelope. It felt as if it contained probably about twenty pieces of paper. I tucked it under my arm.

"It's copies of my dealings with AIM. Perhaps you could look through it?"

"With pleasure," I replied.

Over her shoulder I could see Alan Purdy again glance in my direction. His brow furrowed for a fleeting second as he saw us talking. He turned and made a quick remark to a younger man standing beside him. The man flicked a look towards us and nodded. He immediately detached himself from the group and, accompanied by one of his colleagues, came purposefully over to us.

"Mrs Hetherington, nice to see you here," said the colleague, taking her by the arm and leading her away from me.

At the same time the other man addressed himself to me. Looking at my name badge which I had not yet had time to hand in he said, "Mr Bruce, may I introduce myself. David Firkin. I work for Mr Purdy at AIM. I hope you enjoyed the conference."

It was clearly a manoeuvre planned to break up our little conversation. My guess was that Purdy didn't want me talking to Alice. The question was "Why?".

Chapter 7

It was immediately clear to me that Purdy had sent his henchman over to find out who I was and what, if anything, I thought I was up to. He could not afford to show that he was upset by my question.

"I found it very interesting," I said.

"Are you an investor, or a potential investor?" he asked, looking again at my badge.

"I'm semi-retired," I answered. "I came along because I have several clients whose money I look after. The kind of people that AIM seems to be interested in. So I thought I'd find out what you have to offer."

"Interesting. Have you got ten minutes? I could perhaps give you some more insight into our approach if you have the time and, if you think it worth it, we could arrange a more formal meeting later. Do you live in Edinburgh?"

"No. I live over in Fife in a small village called Letham. Do you know it?"

"No, I'm afraid not. Look, we have some meeting rooms here. Why don't we take five minutes if you're not in a hurry?"

It was a good salesman's pitch and I decided to go along with it. Perhaps I'd learn a bit more.

Firkin's colleague had by now joined us, having helped Alice on her way and we repaired to a small meeting room just off the lobby.

The room had been set up for just such eventualities. There was a table in the centre with six chairs around it. There was a jug of coffee, cups and biscuits on a buffet standing against the wall. The view from the window down Princes Street was magnificent.

"Coffee? Let's sit down."

Firkin's colleague, who was so far nameless, pulled out a chair for me and I took my place. He sat down opposite me and Firkin brought us three coffees. "No Name" looked about thirty. He was fairly big and muscular and, although he was dressed as all the others in a grey suit, shirt and tie, none of these things looked as if they belonged to him. He didn't look like a young investment banker. He seemed to me more like a scrubbed up truck driver. But then appearances can be misleading, as Dad had always told me.

We chatted generally for a while. Firkin gave me the pitch about the personal approach to investing – the fact that AIM specialised in advice to suit individual circumstances. He was smooth, but there was no doubt he was trying to wheedle out of me as much information about myself as he could. How many clients? About a dozen. What kind of investment amounts? On average about a couple of hundred thousand. Where did my clients come from? All over the place – mostly in the country or in smaller towns. I kept away from the big cities.

No Name was taking notes, laboriously. His pen didn't really seem at home in his large hand but he was making a valiant effort.

After about ten minutes I had had enough and said, "I'm afraid I'll have to go now. I have a train to catch in fifteen minutes."

"No problem. It was really nice meeting you and don't hesitate to call me next time you come through to Edinburgh and perhaps we can have lunch and discuss what AIM can do for your clients."

I got up and turned towards the door.

"Just before you go, Mr Bruce …"

I turned back.

"I presume you are who you say you are, but, if by any chance you are not, I would be a bit more careful about the way you ask questions in a public conference."

Firkin said this with a smile. No Name had stood up, towering above his colleague by a good six inches, flexing his fingers after all the unaccustomed note-taking he had been doing. There was no smile on his face.

"That sounds rather like a threat to me."

"Just some friendly advice."

"Thank you," I said and left the meeting room.

The lobby was practically empty by now but I did see Purdy sitting in an armchair in the corner talking earnestly to Gavin Reid, the lawyer I'd met through Keith. I noticed them but made sure that they didn't realise I had seen them.

On the drive home I thought over what had happened that day and promised myself to call Alice and get a decent chance to speak to her.

Pierre and I had agreed that we would have supper together and compare our impressions of the day. I had invited him round to the house and, not being the best of cooks, decided on a carry out Indian meal from the Rajput in Cupar, which was only five miles away. I figured it would also be fitting as Dad had been a great fan of Indian cuisine.

Pierre arrived, as agreed, about seven and we settled ourselves comfortably in my small dining room with a mountain of spicy food and rice and a few bottles of beer.

Once the edge had been taken off our hunger I asked Pierre about his few days up north. He had had an excellent time. The weather had been fine. He'd played a couple of rounds of golf. He'd visited a couple of distilleries and had brought back two of bottles of whisky for Mike and me. They were in the hotel.

We then got onto the day's events. I told him about Steven and the fact that there might be some comment in the papers the next day.

"Your question was just right," said Pierre. "I was watching Purdy when you delivered the missing three and a half million. I've rarely seen a guy look quite so concerned – and he did not like it one bit."

"I have to admit he recovered rather quickly," I replied.

"Sure. But as far as I'm concerned he definitely showed signs of being very uncomfortable."

As I opened another beer, he asked me if Steven had any background knowledge of AIM.

"No, but he has agreed to do a bit of discreet digging."

Pierre added a few more observations.

"When I joined Purdy afterwards he seemed to be only three quarters there. He was chatting to everyone more or less as normal but you could see that his brain was churning away in the background. I noticed him glance across at you a couple of times."

"I know. I saw it too – especially when I was talking to Steven. Did you see me with the little old lady? She told me before we went in that she was worried about the return she was getting from her investment and that was why she was there. When she came up to me afterwards it didn't take long for Purdy to send over a couple of guys to break up our conversation. Interesting, isn't it? She gave me an envelope of papers to look at and asked me if I could give her a call because she wanted some advice from me. Hold on a minute."

I got up and went through to the sitting room where I had deposited Alice's papers and brought them back to the table.

"Have a look at these and see if they seem familiar to you."

I handed the envelope to Pierre and he pulled out what turned out to be a couple of statements full of numbers and copies of a few letters and standard quarterly news bulletins.

Pierre perused them one by one and handed them over to me.

"Just like the stuff I get," he said.

"Bloody hell," I said, looking at one of the statements. "Are you telling me that they hit you guys with a two and a half per cent management fee as well?"

"Sure. It's standard practice, so I've been told. Mind you who knows if everyone has the same level of management fee? There's potential there for a bit of fiddling."

I did a quick calculation. "At two and a half per cent that's a hundred grand for you," I said.

"I know," Pierre replied ruefully. "Not funny is it?"

I grabbed a piece of paper and a pencil.

"Let's see now. If he is buggering about with clients' money and siphoning off, say, three per cent just to be conservative, that's one and a half million on fifty.

If he's taking two and a half per cent management fees as well from everybody that's another one and a quarter million which makes a nice round sum of two and three quarter million quid."

I paused for a second as I did a few more mental calculations.

"And if he's been doing that for the last five years or so that comes to a very useful thirteen point seven five million pounds, less a bit of tax somewhere."

I sat back in my chair and looked across at Pierre.

"Bob, I've told you the money doesn't really mean much to me. For your information I got about ninety million when I sold the company and not too much went on tax. Most of it has been invested sensibly. I don't really have to worry. But," he said, with emphasis, "I do not like being taken for a fool and I don't like crooks, especially those that prey on the elderly."

"There's another thing."

"What?"

"The two guys that Purdy sent over to break up the chat I was having with Alice wanted to have a little meeting."

"Why?"

"Ostensibly to sell their products to a potential investor."

I then told him about the veiled threat I had received at the end of the meeting.

Pierre's reaction was immediate.

"That does it, then. We need to do something."

"Like what?" I asked.

Pierre thought for a moment.

"Here's what I would like to do. We agreed that we've both got time on our hands. You can't work in the garden and play golf all the time. I'm a bit bored. As far as I'm concerned today was confirmation of my suspicions. We need to see how we can expose the bastard."

I thought this over for a minute. He was right. These kinds of crimes never got investigated properly. One reason was that they were often too difficult to prove. Another was that regulatory authorities seldom had teeth and the police, being more and more short handed and more and more snowed under by paperwork, just didn't have the time. Government by objectives had gone crazy and playing by the rules was a slow process.

We were a couple of old farts who had time on their hands. Pierre could obviously supply financial backing and I had got to the stage in life where bending a few rules to achieve a morally correct objective was not going to bother me one bit.

I summarised this to Pierre and grinned. He lent over the table and stuck out his hand. I took it and thereby committed myself to a course of action which was going to have some startling consequences.

"Let's plan the next steps."

We banged around a few ideas for the space of half an hour. As far as Purdy was concerned I was the thorn in his flesh. Pierre was just a client. We agreed to keep it that way. Our connection would be kept secret.

I would talk to Steven as soon as possible and get him digging on the promise that, whatever came out of it, he would get an exclusive.

I would go and see Alice and find out if she knew any other fellow investors. Meanwhile we should bring Mike into the equation.

"He has contacts from his old army days – guys that can do a bit of following or digging and if we can find out anything that proves that Purdy has a lot more money than he should have we'll have a lever on him."

We agreed to get Mike over the next morning and get things moving.

Pierre left to go back to the hotel and I turned in, reeking of curry and beer. As I dropped off to sleep I thought of Liz. She would definitely approve of what I was doing.

I called Mike the next morning and he agreed to come over and we'd meet at Fernie Castle for a bar lunch.

After we had related to Mike the events of the conference and he was completely up to date on everything he was more than happy to get involved.

"So you want me to see if I can dig up any dirt on Mr Alan Purdy?"

"Can you?" we asked.

"No problem. I have a couple of guys who would be just right. I knew them in the army. Mac lives up near Perth and does freelance house painting which bores him rigid but he likes the freedom it gives him. I'll see if he's free. Can I offer to pay him?"

"I'll organise that," said Pierre.

"There is also Doug, who used to be an explosives expert, but that's beside the point. He can do other things. He can't find work very easily at the moment. He'll be up for a bit of tax-free cash."

The plan was launched. I knew what I was going to do, Mike would organize Mac and Doug and Pierre would stay in the background.

"Right little bunch of musketeers, we are," said Mike, finishing off his beer. "We should call ourselves the Three Musketeers. We need a name. I like names."

"The Three Musketeers is a bit old-fashioned," said Pierre.

"Well, how about The Bruce Brothers?" I said with a grin. "One of my favourite films."

We discarded that as being too frivolous and after bandying about a bunch of alternatives – some of them distinctly unusable in female company – we decided we would be APA Consulting (Athos, Porthos and Aramis).

As we were about to leave I mentioned to Pierre that we had an invitation to go through to visit Heather for lunch on Saturday. He was delighted and we decided that he and I would meet Mike on the way so as to arrive together. Our sister could be a bit daunting on occasions and I preferred the idea of presenting a consolidated front.

Mike had to go back home. He had an appointment in Dundee, he said.

"Which will no doubt result in a new photograph in the living room?" I asked mischievously.

"You never know."
Pierre looked mystified.

I called Alice when I got back home and asked her if I could come over and see her the next day. She promptly suggested that I come for lunch. She would rustle up a salad.

I set off the next morning at ten thirty and drove north at a leisurely pace, over the hills and down into the fertile valley of the Tay. It was sunny and I felt invigorated. I had something to do. My brain was operating again and trying to imagine what we were going to discover.

I have to admit that most of my life had centred around the need to forge a career and look after my family. The idea of having the luxury (the time and the money) to do something to help others – to right a wrong, to punish a wrong doer – in some way or other appealed to me. I had a new purpose.

I skirted the fair city of Perth and drove north. Alice had given me directions to her house once I got to the village. They were simple to follow and I arrived at about a quarter to twelve.

Lunch had been prepared (cold salmon salad) in the little verandah that was tacked onto the back of the cottage. I was offered a sherry. The verandah was neat and tidy and let in lots of light yet protected us from the wind. At this time of year it was an ideal place to sit and chat.

And Alice could chat. In her own home there was none of the nervousness she had displayed when we first met. She explained how she lived, how she busied herself with the affairs of the village. She and her husband had come to live there after he had retired from his production management job with a large American paper-making company. They had been lucky because he had, over the years, accumulated a sizeable number of stock options and they had turned out to be quite valuable when he had cashed them in.

They had had two children – one was living down south (down south meant anywhere on the other side of the English border) and the other had emigrated to Australia.

I let her prattle on through lunch and, when she went through to fix some coffee I thought to myself what a nice little old lady she was, although she was probably only about ten years older than me. That Purdy was stealing from her was, in my book, disgusting.

When she brought back the coffee we turned to the subject of her investments and AIM.

"That man is definitely a crook," she announced. "I watched him when you were asking about the 'missing millions'. He's a crook, there's no question about it. I can feel it."

I smiled at this conclusion which was uttered with such conviction, yet based on little more than female intuition as far as I could tell. But over the years I have discovered that female intuition can be a pretty powerful tool.

"I suspect you're right but we can't condemn the man without proof."

"Why not?" she shot back. "A crook's a crook."

"Alice, we don't know yet for sure if he is. That he might be is all we can say at the moment. I and the friend I told you about feel that there is definitely something suspicious and we've decided to see if we can find out for sure."

"That's good." She was clearly excited about the idea that this man would get his just desserts.

"So, in the meantime, what do I do about my money?"

"I'd move it, if I were you," I replied. "I can put you in touch with a good trustworthy financial advisor who will plan a proper investment strategy for you. But talk to him first before you move it. Let him handle that. He's used to it. There may be ways around the penalty clauses. If there are, he'll find them. What you can do for the moment is write to AIM and ask them how much you would get if you cashed in everything now. Just tell them that you have some important costs coming up and you might need to free up your cash. So you need to know how much you would get back if you sold out.

That will serve two purposes – you'll be able to show their reply to Jack Thomson, who is the financial advisor, and also it might get Mr Purdy worried. After all, he didn't like my question and he saw us chatting together after the meeting. He'll probably put two and two together."

That was how, sitting quietly in a verandah in a little village in Perthshire, I stuck a red hot poker into a hornet's nest – but I didn't know it at the time.

I gave her Jack's phone number and she agreed to do what I had suggested. I told her I would keep the copies of her paperwork and asked her to send me a copy of whatever reply she received from AIM.

Before I left I asked Alice if she knew of any other people who were AIM investors.

"Only one," she told me, and gave me a name and address in Perth. A David MacLean.

"He's an old colleague of my husband's. They worked for the same company. He retired a few years before Malcolm. But he must be about ninety by now, if he's still alive."

I thanked her for the lunch, promised to keep in touch and set off back home.

During the journey home I wondered how I might be able to track down other Alices or Davids. If APA was going to achieve anything we were going to need as much knowledge as we could dig up. Perhaps Steven would have an idea.

Chapter 8

I picked up Pierre at the hotel on Saturday morning and we drove through to Doune for our lunch appointment. I took him the more picturesque route through Glendevon.

The Ochil Hills stretch across that part of Scotland from North Fife to Stirling. They form a natural barrier to the Highlands farther north and Glendevon is one of the few roads piercing them. Driving through the glen is the quickest way to get a feel for the rugged wild country farther north. The road twists its way through the glen and comes out into the last low-lying countryside before you hit the mountains. From the shadow of the steep-sided glen we emerged into blue skies stretching to the north where the ominous grey shapes of the mountains filled the horizon.

We came out at the main road from Perth to Stirling, crossed it, and a few minutes later entered the famous golfing domain of Gleneagles, where we had agreed to meet Mike.

We stopped for enough time for a coffee and to show Pierre what a real golf course looked like. He was completely taken by the magnificent surroundings and we promised we would bring him over to play sometime soon.

We left Gleneagles in the two cars and proceeded towards Doune. Mike had announced that he would have to get back fairly early, because, he told me with a grin, he had "to pick up a photograph".

The old grey farmhouse stood on the south-facing slope of a small hill. It was protected from the east wind by a copse of trees. We were on the southern fringe of the Highlands. In the distance were the mountain peaks of varying shades of grey and blue, eventually fading with the distance until they merged into the sky.

There were no crops in the surrounding fields. This was not an arable farm. Oliver, my brother-in-law, raised cattle for the meat industry. The fields were grass, populated by young cows, which he bought regularly at the local sales, fattened them up for a year or so and then sold them on to the meat-packing industry. It was a profitable enough business and it had the advantage of not being very labour intensive. He ran about three hundred cattle, buying and selling three or four a week except during the winter when he depleted his stock with sales, and built it up again during the spring.

During the cold months, when the cattle were inside, he needed a young lad to help with the feeding, but other than that he could run the whole place single handed. There had, however, never been very much opportunity for holidays when the kids had been small. Perhaps that is why they had both chosen other careers.

The life suited Heather who had always had a few horses. It was permanently busy but there was little in the way of the stress of city life, the professional politics and the bloody traffic that I had had to put up with all my life.

I had explained all this to Pierre as we had driven through and he was looking forward to meeting them.

I rang the door bell and was immediately rewarded by a pile of noises from inside the house. I say "a pile" because they all seemed to me to be stacked on top of each other.

"I'll get it" – thump of running feet – "Get off" – "I'm first" – a crash of something falling over – a clunk on the inside of the door – the noise of the handle being wrenched open.

The door was hauled back to reveal two grinning, perspiring faces – Rory, ten and Paddy (Patrick), eight – Heather's grandsons.

"Hi, Uncle Bob," they cried in unison. "Hi, Uncle Mike."

"Hi, scamps," I replied, ruffling their hair. Mike's welcome was more violent. He lunged forwards and grabbed them both, one under each arm, and promptly turned round and walked over to the pile of grass clippings against the wall and unceremoniously dropped the two squealing boys into it.

"Hi guys," he said with a grin, and came back to us, rubbing his hands. "That'll keep them quiet for a while."

Oliver came to the door to welcome us. Looking round he saw his two grandsons emerging, covered in grass clippings and, with a wink to us, roared at them, "What the blazes do you two think you're up to?"

"It was him," they cried, pointing fingers at Mike who was looking a picture of innocence.

"Me? Nonsense."

"Get yourselves cleaned up before you come back in the house."

They scampered off round the corner, grinning at each other.

Oliver ushered us in through the hall and into the kitchen which was at the back of the house.

Heather looked up and smiled at us from behind a pile of kitchen utensils and food, spread out all over the place. She was in the middle of preparation for lunch.

"Hi guys, you're early. I haven't finished all this yet." She waved her arms vaguely over the work in progress, a wicked looking knife in her hand. "Why don't you go out the back and Oliver will get you a drink. I'll be out in a minute."

"Out the back" was a stone-flagged terrace with a large

teak table and eight chairs looking out over a small pond off to the left and a view across the carse to the mountains in the distance. The pond was the territory of a few ducks that were gliding around on the surface of the water.

Pierre had followed along behind and before we sat down I introduced him to Oliver as a friend who was staying at Fernie Castle and whom I had met at the golf club.

I had decided to break the news to Heather alone to give her a chance to absorb the shock on her own, rather than in front of Pierre.

I agreed to the beer suggested by Oliver and went back in to see Heather. She was just washing her hands, having finished whatever it was she had been doing. I went over, gave her a hug and signaled her to sit down for a minute.

"So the surprise friend is not female," she said with a grin. "You had me wondering."

"No, not female. French, in fact. I'll introduce him to you in a minute."

Oliver wandered through clutching several bottles of beer. "We'll be out in a few minutes," I called.

"Take your time."

I then proceeded to tell my wee sister about the unexpected visitor I had had the previous week, the dinner we had together and the astonishing news. She listened to the whole story without a word of interruption. When I had finished she looked at me closely.

"You're kidding, aren't you?"

"Absolutely not. It's all true. You can even see a family resemblance from time to time."

"And you believe this story from someone turning up out of the blue?"

"I really do – and he's a nice guy. Mike and I have got to know him over the last week and we've had a chance to get used to the idea. I have to admit it was a bit of a shock at first. But when you think about, it doesn't seem an unreasonable story. Apparently he's not the only person in France of that generation who didn't know his father. I'm telling you, when he put that photo down on the table in front of me I was completely astounded. It's a smaller version of exactly the same one as you've got hanging in your dining room."

We explored the business from all angles for a few minutes until Heather seemed to me to be convinced. Finally she got up and said, "Well, I suppose I'd better go and meet him."

Mike, Oliver and Pierre had migrated over to the duck pond and were chatting amiably, glasses in their hands. They turned as we approached. Pierre must have guessed that Heather had been told. He looked at her rather nervously.

She walked slowly up to him, her keen eyes taking in everything about him. She paused about three feet away, cleared her throat, swallowed and then said in a soft voice, "Bob has just told me."

Her lips quivered and her eyes started to water. She took a step forward, put her arms round him and said "Welcome."

She let go of him after a few seconds and stepped back. "It's a bit of a shock, as you can well imagine, and it's going to take some getting used to. Come on. Put your beer down and let's go for a short walk. The lunch can wait a bit. It's cold stuff anyway."

She took him by the arm and walked off down the driveway.

Oliver clearly wondered what the hell was going on. He looked at me questioningly, then at Mike, then at his wife and this stranger wandering off down the drive talking to each other.

"Could someone tell me what is going on?"

Just then there was a shriek from the house, followed by the emergence of two young boys from the kitchen door dressed in swimming shorts. They pelted past us and plunged into the pond to the vocal disapproval of the sitting tenants. The ducks took off noisily and the boys had the water to themselves.

I looked at Mike. "Why don't you go off for a short wander and explain to Oliver. I'll look out for the boys."

Mike nodded his agreement and he and Oliver went off with their beers in the direction of the horse field. I was left to sit on the bench and babysit while I awaited the return of the family.

When all four had returned and before we all sat down to lunch we agreed that it wouldn't be right to tell the kids. Heather would organise breaking the news to their mother first.

Lunch was jovial. The food was, as always, excellent. The Pouilly Fuissé was deliciously cold. Jokes about the French cropped up. The kids were boisterous but also curious about a country they had never visited and peppered Pierre with questions which he handled with good humour. He was clearly interested in them and gave as good as he got. Vague plans were discussed about going out to France, although we had not yet mentioned how rich our new brother was.

I was quieter than usual and was more interested in watching Pierre slip into an affectionate relationship with my family. All in all things had gone even better than I had hoped. Pierre was delighted with his new-found sister. After we had finished eating she took him to show him round the farm and introduce him to the horses.

By the middle of the afternoon Mike had left for his evening rendezvous and Oliver, Pierre, Heather and I carried on chattering until Heather proposed that we stay for supper. The main subject was of course Dad and we were able to add still more of the picture to Pierre. He was also able to tell what he knew about that year in France from what he had heard from his mother. We knew almost nothing of that period in Dad's life.

I drove a very happy Pierre back through to Fife and deposited him at his hotel. We agreed to get together the next day. I still had to tell him about my visit to Alice.

The next morning I was obliged to call Pierre earlier than anticipated.

"Hi, it's Bob. Morning. Sorry to bother you but could you come over this morning? I think I've had a break in at home."

"What?"

"I said that I think someone has been in my house – presumably while we were away yesterday. Can you come over?"

"That sounds crazy. Has anything been taken?"

"I don't think so. That's what's so strange."

"Hold on. I'll be with you in three quarters of an hour."

He arrived fifty minutes later. During the time I was waiting for him I had gone over the house a second time to make sure that nothing was missing. I saw his car draw up outside and went to let him in. He entered, looking concerned. I offered him a drink. While I was pouring a beer he looked around the downstairs looking puzzled.

"If nothing is gone, how do you know there's been a break in? How did they get in?"

"I haven't a clue. There are no broken windows or bust locks or anything. If I'm right they were professionals."

"What do you mean nothing? How do you know someone's been in here then?"

I explained how, when I had got up and was having my breakfast, I suddenly had a feeling that there was something strange about the house.

"I couldn't put my finger on it but it troubled me. When I was putting the breakfast things away I noticed a leaf lying on the floor in the kitchen. I absentmindedly picked it up to put it in the rubbish. Then I thought, wait a minute, that's queer. I'm normally very fastidious about brushing my feet when I come in the back door from the garden. How the hell did this leaf get there? I'm sure it wasn't there yesterday when I left. I'm sure I would have noticed it."

"So, what then?" asked Pierre.

"I had a look around. Everything seemed normal, but …"

I then explained to him how I had gone back into the living room. I had stood in the middle of the floor and scanned the room slowly. It had seemed as usual.

"But you get used to certain things being in certain places when you live on your own. And you know that you're the only person that can move things."

"That I understand," said Pierre.

"I have one particular hang up which always used to annoy Liz. I hate pictures that are not exactly horizontal. Sometimes I even check them with a spirit level. Liz thought I was daft but it's always been something that disturbs me. I've even been known, much to her embarrassment, to straighten pictures in other people's houses, or tell the proprietor of a restaurant that his pictures are squint."

"What did you notice?"

"Dad's picture, on the wall leading towards the kitchen, was not quite right and that big oil over there of Glencoe that Liz gave me for our twenty-fifth wedding anniversary was definitely on a slant. How the hell could that have happened?"

I then described to Pierre how slowly the idea had started to percolate into my brain that someone had come into the house while I was out and had been snooping around. Impossible. Crazy. But what if it was true?

I had gone straight to the front door to check if there were any signs of illicit entry. Nothing. I had checked all the windows – upstairs and downstairs. Nothing. The back door, which led off from the kitchen seemed unmolested.

I had concluded that I must be imagining things. Old age catching up with me. Bullshit. I still had all my marbles.

"I even went out the front door and crossed the road to look back at the house, to see if there was anything unusual. All seemed as you would expect it to be. I walked up the lane at the side of the house and looked over into the garden. Still nothing different. The only thing I did notice were fresh-looking car tyre tracks on the verge, as if a car had stopped there. There could be a perfectly logical explanation for that, although not many cars go up the lane because it only leads to Jack Gibson's farm a mile and a half further on."

"Let's do another check," suggested Pierre

We started upstairs but without any result.

We went back into the living room. It was then that I noticed that one of the drawers in the hall table was not properly shut.

"Pierre, look here," I called him over.

"This drawer isn't properly shut. It needs some sanding so that it'll close smoothly and neatly. I've been meaning to fix it for months but I've never got round to it. As it is, it needs a special technique. You have to push it closed on the left side first. It is a bit of a fiddle to do but I always do it because it looks untidy otherwise."

Pierre tried to close it without success.

If you didn't take the time to find out the technique it would remain partly open at one side. That was the giveaway. Someone had definitely been in my house. I then started to look much more carefully. There were hardly any signs. Whoever it was had been extremely professional and careful. Practically nothing had been disturbed – practically nothing, but not nothing.

The pictures, the leaf, the drawer – and I noticed also that a wooden box that I kept papers in had been slightly displaced. There were signs in the dust that it had been moved. My cleaning lady only comes in once a week and although she's good with a vacuum cleaner and she's got a thing about clean windows, she's not too hot on the dusting, bless her.

Pierre was thoughtful as I pointed out the evidence to him.

"If you're right and someone has been in, why didn't they take anything?"

All I could think of as an answer was that there wasn't much of value in the house anyway.

"Could they have been looking for a document or documents? That fits with looking behind pictures."

"I don't have any documents of any importance. Anything like that I keep in the safe deposit box at the bank."

I stopped suddenly. Documents. "Shit!"

"What is it?" asked Pierre.

"Alice's envelope."

"What do you mean?"

"The documents that Alice Hetherington gave me at the conference. All her papers concerning AIM – the stuff I showed you the other evening. I put the envelope down on the bureau over there and, as it is not something that's usually here, I've only just realised that it is missing. I know I put it down there on Friday evening when I got back."

"Why would anyone think that papers in a brown envelope would have any value?" asked Pierre.

"God knows."

We looked at each other, both coming to the realisation at the same time.

"It can only be Purdy or someone sent by him. He saw Alice give me the envelope ..."

"... which means," went on Pierre, "that they are important, at least to him, and he doesn't want anybody poking his nose into one of his client's correspondence ..."

"... which means he has something to hide ..."

"... which means that we're maybe right and there definitely is something fishy about AIM," I said, finishing off the combined train of thought.

Chapter 9

As it was warm and sunny we went out into the back garden and sat down on my patio. I looked ruefully at the garden which definitely needed some attention. For a start the rose beds were becoming overgrown with weeds. I hated the task. Down on your hands and knees wrestling with dandelions, chickweed and daisies, which had somehow migrated from the small patch of grass that I had. I told myself I would have to do something about it within the next few days.

I told Pierre about my visit to Alice and how, unfortunately, she only knew of one other person who had invested in AIM. I thought I might try to contact him.

"I wish there was some way we could get hold of the names of more people. Perhaps that would give us more information."

"What about Alice?" Pierre asked.

"What do you mean?"

"Can you get her to recopy her papers and send them over? We might discover what it was that Purdy found so important."

I was struggling with the cork of a bottle of Beaujolais when Pierre spoke again.

"Bob, I've just had another thought. If these papers of Alice are so important and Purdy sees that they are copies, do you think he might try to get hold of the originals?"

"Bloody hell. I didn't think of that."

I finally got the cork out and poured us each glass. The wine had been in the fridge and was deliciously cool.

"We'd better warn her."

"What about putting a guard on over there?" suggested Pierre.

That seemed to make sense because if anyone did try to do another burglary on Alice's house a guard might catch him in the act. We'd have a way of confirming who was behind it and something to nail him with.

"Can you fund the cost?"

"No problem."

I got on the phone to Mike, who answered with a "morning after the night before" voice.

I told him about the break-in and the disappearance of Alice's papers and explained our concern about a repetition on Alice's house.

"Have you contacted Doug and Mac yet?" I asked.

"Yes. They're up for it. I'm seeing them tomorrow to give them a rundown and send them over to Edinburgh."

"Good. Can you change the plan a bit? Would Mac be able to go and babysit Alice for a few days? Our idea was that we would offer to repaint the outside of her house for free and she could put Mac up for the three or four days that it would take and be bodyguard at the same time. Maybe nothing will happen but you never know. And you and Doug could do the Edinburgh side of things."

He agreed and promised to organise it like that. I gave him Alice's name and address and said I would phone her straight away. He could assume all was on if he didn't hear from me. That way I'd save the price of a phone call.

Next, Alice.

She was horrified when I told her about the break in.

"Told you so. That man is definitely a crook."

I then explained how we were concerned that they might pay her a visit as well, so we planned to supply some security. I had no trouble persuading her to accept a repainting job on the outside of her house, free of charge. She was a Scot after all. And she agreed that she could put Mac up for the few days it would take, on condition that he was a non-smoker. I assured her that he was although I hadn't a clue. I was going to have to phone back Mike after all.

Once that was all settled Pierre and I reviewed the situation. There was not much we could do over the next few days. Mac would be guarding Alice. Mike and Doug would be investigating Purdy. And I would have a chat with Steven in a couple of days to see if he had found out anything.

His article in the Thursday paper had been just right. A brief report of the conference with no reference to the awkwardness caused by my question. It was neutral on the issue of AIM's results, which would not please Purdy very much. But he couldn't complain. It was factual.

Pierre was quiet and thoughtful as I did my little "where we're at" speech.

He left me in the early afternoon. As he was leaving he informed me that, as not much was likely to happen in the near future, he was going to go back to France for a few days. He would be back on Wednesday or Thursday. He didn't tell me why. But then why should he? I simply nodded and asked him to call when he got back.

Nothing happened over the next few days. I called Alice a couple times. She was delighted with the painting. She and Mac had agreed on an olive green for the woodwork, which she thought would brighten things up and would go well with all the shrubs and trees she had in the garden.

I spoke to Mac who had nothing to report except that he was eating like he hadn't done in a long time. Alice was spoiling him and was clearly enjoying having someone to cook for. His only complaint was that he had to play Scrabble every evening and she always won.

I tried to get in touch with Steven but his assistant told me he was out of town and wouldn't be back until the end of the week.

I managed a round of golf. I went over on Tuesday and bumped into Keith in the clubhouse. He was about to go out with Jack and he invited me to join them. I played reasonably well. Jack was not on form with his putting and Keith thumped his way round the course, cursing bad shots, complaining about the greens when he missed a putt and celebrating as if he'd won the Open when anything went in from over ten feet.

On Thursday morning I had a call from Mike who suggested that he come over and report on his and Doug's efforts over the last three days. We agreed to a bar lunch at Fernie. He'd come over himself and leave Doug on the job.

Just as I was about to leave the phone rang again. It was Pierre.

"Hi," he said. "What's new? I'm just back and wondered if you fancied lunch."

I told him I was meeting Mike so his arrival was well timed. We'd see him in about half an hour.

Mike was waiting in the bar. No sign, as yet, of Pierre, so we settled down for a debriefing on Edinburgh.

We had hardly started when Mike glanced up and said "Here's Pierre".

I looked round over my shoulder and saw Pierre wending his way through the chairs and tables towards us with a smile on his face. He was dressed in his usual tidy, elegant way – blue, cotton, neatly-ironed trousers, soft brown loafers, fresh cream shirt. His face was, if anything slightly more tanned than before. A couple of days in the sun, I thought.

Mike and I glanced at each other. Mike raised his eyebrows. We had been expecting him but we had not been expecting him to be accompanied.

We got to our feet as he approached and shook hands and welcomed him back.

"Hi, guys. Good to see you," he said and then stepped back to motion forward the person who had been following closely behind.

She was a distinctly attractive lady and looked as if she was in her early forties. She had an open and friendly expression on a face that was tanned and very appealing. She was an inch or so taller than Pierre, slender with shoulder-length black hair and was dressed neatly in a blue cotton blouse and a white denim skirt which stopped just above the knees. Bare legged. Sandals with just enough heel to tighten up the calf muscles. There was no doubt the picture was exquisite. She took a pace forward and shook us each by the hand. There was a whiff of a seriously expensive perfume in the air.

"It's good to meet you both," she said, with a slight touch of a French accent. "Pierre has told me all about you."

Pierre pulled out a seat for her and we all sat down again, Mike taking slightly longer than the rest of us. He couldn't take his eyes off her. She seemed aware of this and smiled back at him.

"Bob, Mike, I'd like to introduce you to Sophie Lamarre, a long-time friend of mine."

We nodded and smiled a welcome to her.

Mike promptly got up to order drinks for the new arrivals.

"Beer for you, Pierre? And Sophie ...?"

"A small glass of cold, dry white wine, please," she said, her eyes following him as he went over to the bar.

Pierre sat back in his chair with a satisfied smile on his face, as if he had made exactly the effect that he had intended. He said something in French to Sophie who laughed out loud, revealing a perfect set of teeth.

There was a definite elegance about her, but also an indication of strength and fitness in that slim body. Someone who looked after herself or someone who enjoyed outside pursuits. The slight tan seemed to indicate the latter.

We chatted for a few minutes as one does when a stranger suddenly arrives in your midst and you want to make them welcome. Have you been to Scotland before? What do you think of the weather? And other such comments.

I tried my best to get the conversation going but I couldn't bring up our Purdy adventures because I didn't really know who she was. Was this Pierre's partner? Could be. They certainly seemed to be very much at ease with each other.

Meanwhile Mike, unusually for him, hardly opened his mouth.

When I started to stall a little Pierre decided to let us off the hook. He murmured again to Sophie in French and received a nod of the head in return.

"Listen guys, we both know what you're thinking. We're used to it. Let me just say straight away that Sophie and I are not, as you say it over here, an 'item'. We are just very good old friends. Most people have the same reaction, which I take as a compliment to my sense of taste. Sometimes we let people think so because it gives Sophie some protection. But this time I have to tell you straight away. I just wanted to have a little fun."

"Well you certainly looked very much like a couple when you came over here," I said. "Pierre, the well-dressed Frenchman, with his beautiful partner" – I can be a charmer when I want to be!

"In France we dress to please the ladies," said Pierre.

Mike grinned and couldn't stop himself from coming out with a rejoinder.

"Over here we undress to please the ladies." Then he realised that he'd perhaps over-stepped the mark, coloured slightly and buried his face in his beer. Sophie was clearly not bothered by this remark and joined the laughter.

Pierre continued. "I hope you guys don't mind but I've invited Sophie over here to help us in our project."

He then proceeded to explain to us that Sophie had worked for his company from just after she had graduated from college and she had been with them until he sold out. She had developed into a top-class IT security and hacking expert. When Pierre had sold the company she had sold the shares that she had accumulated from various bonuses and had set herself up as an independent expert.

"Bob, when you mentioned that it would be good if we could get hold of other AIM investors, I immediately thought of Sophie. Perhaps she can hack into their systems. So I went over to discuss it with her. She has some free time at the moment and said she'd love to help."

"D'Artagnan," said Mike.

"I beg your pardon?" said Sophie, looking puzzled.

We then had to explain to her why we had called ourselves APA Consulting. She liked the idea immediately and accepted to be D'Artagnan.

I readily agreed to the help that Sophie could bring. If she could get into their systems we'd be in an excellent position to unmask Purdy.

Mike agreed for reasons known only to himself – but suspected by me.

Over lunch I called the meeting to order and we reviewed the steps we needed to undertake.

"Sophie, what do you need to be able to get into their systems?"

"Just a simple connection to a server or access to WiFi," she replied.

"Well I've got internet at home, which is only five minutes away. Will that do? Or I'm sure they have WiFi here in the hotel."

"Yours would be better," she replied.

"Fine. Pierre can bring you over tomorrow. It'll give me time to tidy up a bit and clear a space for you to work."

Mike then gave us a report on what he and Doug had found out in Edinburgh.

He showed us photos of Purdy leaving his expensive-looking house in Barnton, arriving at the office, going out for lunch, the AIM building, his top of the range Lexus and then ...

"This is an interesting one," he said. He pulled out another picture. It was of Purdy walking up a street somewhere in the city, not readily identifiable, with a young, shapely blonde woman on his arm. They were obviously talking to each other in a very friendly fashion.

"Why?" we asked.

"She's not his wife."

He pulled out a glossy AIM brochure which had a photograph of a group of people taken at some public event and in the middle of the group was Purdy with a dark-haired lady standing next to him.

"That's his wife," said Mike, pointing to her.

"That's great. Purdy has a mistress. That could be useful. Do you know who she is or where she lives?"

"Yes. We have a name and an address. She is a divorcee and runs a hairdressing salon in the High Street. We've quite a few photographs of her."

"Fine. Keep away from her now. We don't want to run

any risk of her finding out she's being watched. As long as we know how to get to her if we need to."

"Anything else?" asked Pierre.

"We've only managed to come across two blokes who he seems to frequent. He goes to a squash club down in Leith twice a week. He always plays with the same guy. We followed him there on Tuesday and after he'd gone I had a look at the board of court reservation and his name was up every Tuesday and Thursday with the same guy and at the same time. It's obviously regular."

"Who's the guy?"

"Don't know yet," he replied. "We only have a name, Bill Dewar. But I've asked Doug to find out more … just in case."

"And the second person?"

Mike pushed a photo over to me.

"He's lunched twice this week with this man."

I picked it up and looked at it. It was only a three-quarter view and taken through a window but the man looked distinctly familiar.

Then I thought I had it. I pushed the picture across to Pierre.

"Mean anything to you, Pierre?"

He stared at it for while.

"This man was at the conference."

"Correct. I think that's a man called Gavin Reid who could well be AIM's lawyer. Personally I don't much like the look of him. Could you check him out as well, Mike?"

We broke up around three. We agreed that Pierre would bring Sophie round the next morning and, as he hadn't much else to do, he'd go down and play Lundin Links, which I told him was another of Dad's favourite courses.

Mike would be going back to Edinburgh to check up on Gavin Reid and Purdy's squash playing friend, Bill Dewar.

Chapter 10

The next morning I got up early. There hadn't been a woman in the house since Liz died, apart from my cleaning lady and Mrs Clark. There was a distinct male atmosphere to the place. There wasn't much I could do about that but at least I could tidy up a bit.

I opened all the windows to let the air in. Books were tidied away and the place was given a good vacuuming. Checked out the bathroom. Made sure it was presentable and clean. I definitely needed to clean the kitchen. Last night's frying pan lying in the sink was not a good idea.

By the time I'd done all that I was exhausted and my back was aching.

I sat down for a minute and looked at Dad's picture on the opposite wall. I told him a bit more about Pierre, about Mike and Heather's reaction to him and the news that their Dad had a secret past. I told him that we didn't mind in the least. After all, he didn't know anything about Pierre but, "I'm sure that you'd approve of him if you'd met him", I told him.

I cleared the desk where my PC sits to give Sophie some working space.

I realised that I was thinking thoughts about Sophie that I really shouldn't be. Forget it, I told myself. I'm past all that, and she wouldn't be interested. I'm far too old. Sad, but there it is. Liz's picture in the corner seemed to nod approval.

Pierre and Sophie arrived at around ten thirty. Pierre

didn't stay as he had organised an eleven thirty tee-off time.

I showed Sophie around, offered her a cup of coffee and helped her to connect up her laptop.

"I'll leave you to it," I said. "I've got some gardening to do. Make yourself at home and if you need anything just call."

She settled down to do battle with the world wide web and I went out to get on with some pruning and weeding.

I popped in occasionally to check that all was well. Sophie was totally concentrated. She'd pulled her hair back and fixed it with a rubber band behind her head and she had a neat pair of glasses perched on the end of her nose.

The screen of her laptop was showing screeds of numbers, letters or formulae cascading down at a tremendous pace. There were half a dozen discs lying on the table beside her and a pad and a pencil with notes. Whatever she was doing was completely beyond me.

She turned and smiled when she heard me.

"Everything ok?" I asked.

"Sure. But this could take some time."

There was the day (about forty years ago) when I would have said "Take all night if you want", but instead I replied that there was no particular hurry.

I pottered around in the garden for another half hour then went in to suggest to Sophie that she stop for a while and we'd have a bite of lunch. The computer was still crunching numbers at a vast rate.

I proposed some fish pâté and Chablis which I had in the fridge. This was met with approval. We sat outside in the sun, but sheltered from the wind.

Over lunch I learned how she and Pierre had worked

closely together for years. How it was Pierre that had given her her chance to develop. The company had paid for her to have extra training and it had been a great place to work. She had been very sad when Pierre had sold out but she had understood. She obviously had a great affection and respect for my elder brother and they had clearly been good friends as well as colleagues. She knew all about his history and his desire to find out more about his father.

I got up and brought out Dad's picture and showed it to her. She had seen the tiny copy that Pierre had but she was fascinated by the larger framed version.

"Wow," she said. "There's really quite a family resemblance isn't there? You all seem to have something of him in you. With Pierre it's the shape of the head. I can see his mouth and chin in you and that's definitely Mike's eyes."

I told her a bit about myself, my career, Liz's early death and Callum out in Australia. I told her about Heather and something about Mike. Our upbringing and education, which had been so different from France.

She told me how delighted Pierre was at having discovered an unknown family.

"He seems to have been rejuvenated by about ten years. It's great for him."

"And how about you? Where's home? No husband or kids?"

She smiled. "No. Unfortunately – or fortunately, I'm not sure – I found out in my early twenties that I couldn't have children. Most guys want them and I never found anyone that I wanted to see over the breakfast table every morning for the rest of my life. It's no big deal. I can have a bit of fun when I want to and move on when I feel smothered. I've been very successful in my career and have the money to enjoy complete freedom."

Half of me could understand that but the other half, far

larger, thought back with affection to the wonderful years I had had with Liz.

I asked her how she was getting on with the task in hand.

"Slowly," was the reply.

She then proceeded to give me an idiot's course in hacking, explaining about IP addresses, ultra high speed scanning programmes and a whole lot of other technical jargon which was way above my head.

"And they won't know you've been in there?"

"Not if I leave no trace behind."

"And if you do?"

"Well, first of all, they'd have to be pretty good. Most companies use external IT people and they don't give the same service as your own internal people. But if they do find out it'll because I left a trace. Normally you clean out all traces before you leave. But it's not fool proof."

"And could they get back to you?"

"What do you mean?"

"Could they identify where the hacking came from?"

"If I left a trace and they had the software, yes."

Sophie went back to work. I went back to pottering and the afternoon wore on slowly.

About four o'clock I heard Sophie call me. I went in to find her with a very pleased expression on her face.

"I've done it," she said with glee.

She waved a CD at me. I walked over and congratulated her. I took the disc from her hand. It looked pretty innocuous – like any other disc.

"On there is a list of all the investors in the three funds run by AIM and all the information about the funds' investments over the last five years. I haven't looked at the detail yet but it's all there."

"Great," I said and asked her if she'd made another copy.

"Not yet," she said, "But I'll do it right now." She stuck a new disc in the slot on the side of her machine, punched a few buttons. It whirred away for a minute or two and then ejected.

"We've now got two copies on disc and one on the machine. Now give me some quiet while I get rid of all the traces of my visit. It'll take me a good half hour."

I left her to her labours and went to tidy away the tools I had been using outside. Tomorrow we'd be able to have a good look at the inside workings of AIM and get to grips with Mr Purdy's machinations.

Pierre arrived about ten minutes later, full of the joys of his golfing experience. He'd met a couple of members who had invited him to play with them and he had thoroughly enjoyed himself.

We interrupted Sophie to share the news of her success and opened a bottle of wine. We decided to meet the next day and take our time to analyse what we had found.

"Leave one copy here for safety," I said to Sophie, and she put one on the shelf above my computer.

Pierre then got up to leave.

"Come on Sophie, hurry up. Don't forget I promised you a good dinner tonight. Do you want to come along, Bob?"

I declined. "No thanks. I'm going to have a good bath and an early night after all the work I've done outside."

"Sophie, are you not finished yet?"

"Nearly," she said. "Stop hustling me."

Her finger tapping speeded up and a few minutes later she closed the lid of her machine and got up to go.

We decided to leave it with me until tomorrow. I wasn't going to try to read the disc until Sophie came back the next day to show us how. I was scared I might wipe something out.

Hot bath. Meal in front of the TV, watching some European Tour event and then off to bed with a book – a reasonable evening programme for an oldie like me.

We started the next morning just after ten. I had nipped in to Cupar and stocked up with printer ink and paper. I guessed we were going to need it.

Sophie powered up my PC which was linked to the printer and slipped in the disc. The screen was suddenly filled with stacks of file references. Each had names and codes which meant nothing to any of us yet.

We opened up the first one which turned out to be a file of data concerning a certain Michael Baxter. It listed all his personal details – name, birth date, marital status, children, occupation or previous occupation. It turned out he was widowed, seventy-eight years old and lived in Inverness. He had been a veterinary surgeon and had one daughter (details given), who had presented him with two grandchildren. He had invested three years ago and had still two years to run. He had invested a hundred and thirty thousand pounds and had earned a return of three point two per cent which had been paid out to him in the middle of January each year - just over four thousand pounds to add to his pension.

We tried a few other ones. Each file had the same kind of information. There were between two hundred and fifty and three hundred of these files for each of the three funds, which meant an average investment of about a hundred and eighty thousand pounds.

Suddenly Pierre told Sophie to stop for a minute.

"What's that box over there on the left?"

On the left-hand side of the screen there was a framed box with nothing in it. Sophie moved her mouse over it and up flashed a label with the words 'Password Protected'.

We all looked at each other.

"Can you bust the password, Sophie?" I asked.

"Should be able to," she replied. "But it'll take a bit of time."

She pulled a set of discs from her briefcase and stacked them up beside her then proceeded to feed the top one into the slot.

"This could take an hour or two," she told us. "So you two can go and have a walk or something while I work."

Pierre and I took her at her word and went off for an hour up through the village to the hills behind. We walked gently, admiring the view and enjoying the fresh air. As we walked I pointed out some of the landmarks and gave him a brief history lesson about the area.

We returned after an hour and a half and I made us all a cup of coffee. I was in the middle of explaining to Pierre the history of Falkland and its palace when Sophie called through to us. She had found the password and could now show us what was written in the box.

For the particular file we had on the screen it said 'Admitted retirement home March 2011. Trustee solicitors MacLean and Padgett, Stonehaven'.

We went back over some more files looking for other comments. There was one where the comment was 'Careful, ex-accountant' and another with 'diagnosed dementia'.

Pierre then spotted something else – not everyone in the same fund was receiving the same rate of return. There seemed to be a correlation between the rates and the comments. Where 'careful' was noted, the return was higher than the poor guy who had dementia. Those in the hands of trustees seemed to be somewhere in the middle.

We sat back and looked at each other, horrified. They were systematically adjusting the rates according to his perceived danger of someone kicking up a fuss.

"Can you guys pull all this information out on to a spreadsheet so that we can really see the overall picture?"

"Sure. No problem."

"Let's do it then. I'll leave you to it. I'm going outside to think about this."

I poured myself a stiff whisky, even if it was before noon, and went out into the garden. I was shocked to the core. I couldn't believe that anyone could mount a scheme so brutally fraudulent and think he could get away with it. But the evidence was there. He must be creaming off millions.

How did he get it past the authorities? The answer must be that he had crooked accountants and lawyers that he paid to turn a blind eye. The authorities would accept what was lodged with them and as long as nobody blew the whistle he was printing money. He had carefully selected his target group so that it was unlikely that anybody would challenge him.

Inside the company I suppose a few people must be in on it but he would probably have sectioned off the work amongst different departments so that no one saw the whole picture.

I went back in after ten minutes to see how Sophie and Pierre were getting on.

"OK you geniuses, where are we?"

Pierre pointed to the screen.

"We've got a spreadsheet for each fund, listing all the investors and all their details. We can sort them by any characteristic you want. Watch."

He called up a menu screen, made a few selections and the whole list sorted itself out into ascending reported rate of return for 2011. All the other characteristics automatically sorted themselves out as well. Hey, presto! All the people in the low percentages had comments indicating that there was little chance of complaints – dementia, deceased, estate awaiting probate, etc. Down at the bottom were all the 'careful', ex-bankers and the like. They had the best returns.

"Pierre, there's your proof if ever you need it. This guy should go to jail."

"I fully agree, but I don't want Sophie to go to jail as well," he replied.

"What do you mean?"

"What Sophie has done is highly illegal. We can't use this stuff. She'd get arrested immediately. We can't publish it either or we'd get sued for millions."

"Well we have to do something," I retorted. "We can't let this bastard get away with this. Let me have a think about it. Can you find out what they really did with these funds and how much they were actually making? If we can get a rough fix on that, then deduct what they have paid out, we'll get an idea of the difference."

"Sure, but it'll take us a couple of days."

"How about getting it worked out by Monday?"

Pierre looked at Sophie who nodded.

"Let's get on with it then," he said.

Pierre was right, I realised. We had proof but we had no usable proof. We couldn't even run the risk of showing this to any of the investors. They would be mad as hell and wouldn't be able to keep quiet about the source of their information. I imagined what Alice would do if I showed her this. She'd probably write to her MP and then we'd be in trouble.

I swiftly came to the conclusion that we were going to need some kind of plan which had nothing to do with the law of the land but which would scupper Purdy and his gang of thieves. The thought of acting outside the law didn't bother me one bit. I considered it a perk of old age.

I needed to think up something and I also needed

Pierre and Mike to agree with it. Mike was still in Edinburgh but had promised to report back here on Sunday.

It could wait until then.

Chapter 11

Mike arrived mid-morning and I updated him on the results of Sophie's hacking and yesterday's afternoon of digging. He was as disgusted as we were about what was going on and agreed that something had to be done.

He told me what had been going on in Edinburgh.

Purdy had had another lunch with Gavin Reid, the slimy lawyer, and they had identified the squash partner.

"It turns out that Bill Dewar is a Scottish MP. He represents an outlying Edinburgh constituency and is a Scottish Nationalist. Used to be Labour but changed his allegiance about five years ago.

"He lives in a terraced house on the outskirts of Linlithgow. I found someone who knows him and got him talking. He didn't think much of him. He used to be a trade unionist and seems to have spent most of his career trying to climb up the political ladder using whatever means that happened to be useful at the time. His Dad was a miner and he left school at fifteen – not that there is anything wrong with that as such – but if he was a waster when he was young he apparently hasn't improved, according to my source. I've left Doug to follow him around for a few days and report back."

At that point the phone rang.

"That'll be Doug," said Mike and went to answer it, explaining that he'd given my number to him in case he had any news.

I could hear a voice on the other end of the line but couldn't make out what was being said. Mike's face had a look of astonishment painted on it.

"What in the hell are you doing in Alicante?" he said, with an air of disbelief.

He listened for a few minutes and then told Doug to dig for as much information as he could find and then follow the guy back. "Give me a call when you get back." He hung up.

"That was Doug," he said as he sat down again. "Apparently our ex-Labour, SNP MP flew out to Alicante yesterday evening. Doug managed to buy a ticket and get on the same plane. He was picked up at the airport by a woman driving a Porsche. Doug managed to get a taxi and he followed them to a bloody great villa not far out of town on the cliffs overlooking the Med. According to Doug the place looks as if it's worth a few million. As you heard, I told him to keep digging and report back when he returned."

"So we've now got a fraudster running an investment company who plays squash twice a week with an MP who lives in a terraced house in Linlithgow and goes out to Spain on a Friday night to stay in a multimillion pound villa…"

Mike broke in. "He only took a small bag as hand luggage, by the way."

"… and a slimy-looking lawyer that he seems to have lunch with a couple of times a week."

"And our fraudster has a mistress."

"And he's prepared to do a bit of burglary," I added.

"Do you think that Purdy, for some reason or another, is passing some of the money to Dewar who is stashing it away in Spain?"

"Could be, but I can't think why."

"Perhaps Dewar knows about the girlfriend and is blackmailing him," suggested Mike.

"Possible. If that house is Dewar's the money must have come from somewhere."

"And our lawyer friend?"

"Don't know."

We gave up surmising and I told him that Pierre and Sophie had gone back to the hotel and would be working on the files. We were invited to go round and eat with them later.

Mike got up. "I'll go round now and see how they're getting on," and headed for the door.

"Tell them I'll be around about half past seven," I called at his retreating back. He replied with something that I didn't catch, got into his car and roared off.

I drove across to the hotel, arriving there at the appointed hour and went into the bar. I found Pierre on his own at a table in the corner.

"Where's Sophie? And Mike? He said he was coming over."

"He did," replied Pierre with a smile and a small shake of the head. "He arrived about an hour ago, decided that we were working Sophie much too hard and promptly took her off to dinner somewhere else."

"Oh, God. Typical. He can't keep away from them."

"She seemed quite keen on the idea. Asked me if I minded. I told her to go ahead. It was nothing to do with me."

"Well she's certainly a cut above his usual," I said "I hope she knows what she's doing. He's going to be sixty in a year and a half."

"So what? Didn't you still feel quite young when you were fifty-eight?"

I thought back and smiled to myself at a few memories.

"And perhaps she makes him feel five years younger? That would make him fifty-three. Sophie's just turned forty-four. So where's the problem?"

"Looks like it's just you and me then. Let's go and eat and decide what we're going to do about our Mr Purdy."

A Tournedos Rossini, a bottle of Nuits St Georges and a malt with our coffee did wonders for my feeling of well-being. We had a complicated picture that was emerging and neither of us knew where it was leading, nor what we were going to do about it, so we just chatted and enjoyed each other's company.

I heard more about Pierre's upbringing in France after the war, about how he had started his company and how it had grown over the years. I filled in more of the story of our family which he absorbed with eagerness. There was no rancour or bitterness in him. He told me that there had been times when he was young when he'd felt it hard not knowing who his father was but he had become much more philosophical about as he got older. He had made a success of his life in spite of the difficult beginnings and, when he eventually found out the truth, he felt no hard feelings towards Dad, who had, after all, known absolutely nothing about his existence.

He confessed to being genuinely delighted to have found us and was looking forward to his later years being much more fulfilling than he had imagined that they might be.

Mike and Sophie arrived back about eleven o'clock and joined us for coffee. They seemed to have become very comfortable in each other's company. Mike was being quite the gentleman and Sophie's warmth of reaction and the easy banter between them made me glance at Pierre with upraised eyebrows. He answered with a smile and a Gallic shrug. Neither Mike nor Sophie noticed our exchange. They were much too interested in each other.

"Time to go," I announced when we had finished our coffee. "Pierre and Sophie have got work to do tomorrow."

Sophie turned to Pierre and asked him something in French which I couldn't follow. There was a bit of gesticulating of hands and a questioning expression on Sophie's face. Pierre raised his eyebrows for a moment, asked another question and got his answer. It seemed to me that she was trying to persuade him into something but I had no idea what it was.

Mike meanwhile had turned to me.

"Mind if I stay the night, Bob?" he asked me.

"My pleasure. Are you going back to Edinburgh tomorrow?"

"Well, no actually. I'm taking the day off."

Pierre then spoke. "And so is Sophie, apparently," he said to me. I looked from one to the other, puzzled.

"I'm taking Sophie to see a bit of Scotland. We're going up to Loch Tay. All she's seen so far is Letham which is not exactly the only part of the country worth seeing."

"What about the analysis we need done?"

"I'll take care of that," said Pierre "I should be able to get through it all tomorrow. Let the young ones have a tourist day if they want."

They both looked slightly embarrassed. I didn't know Sophie that well yet but I did know my brother. This was definitely a different Mike from the one I was used to.

Pierre and I got up to go. Mike and Sophie exchanged a word or two. We all said our "goodnights" and Mike and I set off home.

No sooner were we in the car than Mike looked across at me with a grin.

"No bloody comments from you about photograph collections. Right?"

"I wouldn't dare. Let's go."

I was actually secretly quite glad about the way things were turning out, although I wasn't going to admit it yet. It smelled very much as if Mike had fallen for this delightful Frenchwoman and, hopefully, she for him. I let these thoughts occupy me on the short drive home and avoided making any humorous remarks. Getting on the wrong side of Mike can be dangerous sometimes.

Mike set off the next morning and I decided to get stuck into the information that we had extracted from the AIM files. I fired in the CD and started scrolling through the files, checking the information with the spreadsheet that Sophie had generated. When I was satisfied that everything seemed to have been picked up I closed down all the detailed files and started to concentrate on the spreadsheet. It was much easier to comprehend what had been going on.

I had a file for each of the three funds. Each contained between two hundred and fifty and three hundred names. There were about twenty columns for each name, finishing with the column which contained the comments. I immediately made a copy of each one to work with and closed down the originals.

Where to start?

They were, at the moment, ranked by ascending rate of return so that the poor investors who had received the smallest returns were at the top. There were exceptions, but generally speaking you could see that all the widows over seventy were up in the top third.

Down in the bottom third I found the profiles where the husband and wife were both still alive. They tended to be younger and often the husband had been a banker or an accountant or a lawyer – the type of people who would have a better understanding of numbers. And presumably the fact that both spouses were still alive multiplied the chances of suspicion.

I was totally disgusted at the callousness of the scheme. If you were a widow, eighty-five years old and had been in a retirement home for the last four years, there you were in the top quartile. If you had had a job which had needed an understanding of figures, there you were down near the bottom, coded "careful". At what point you were moved up the rankings to "normal" or then up to "no problem" I hated to think. The whole scheme was cynical in the extreme.

The commentary box noted dates of death of spouses and dates of going into homes. "No children" moved you up the ranks, presumably because there wouldn't be anyone to complain after you'd gone. There were even a few dates shown where someone had been diagnosed with dementia. They must have a staff of people tracking the personal circumstances of each of their investors.

I looked for Alice. She was ranked in the normal section. I found Pierre around the middle as well, presumably because he was French. There were a few foreign names, but not many. They were all in the normal section. My guess was that they would be more difficult to track. All in all it was a picture of utter greed.

The next question was to estimate the differential between what this money had really earned and the amount Purdy had grudgingly passed on to his investors. That would have to wait until Pierre had finished his work.

Whatever the amount was I had proof, right in front of me, of the fraud.

I took a break and rustled up a cup of coffee. I'd been looking at these numbers for a couple of hours and the old eyes needed a rest.

I thought things over for five minutes. Purdy knew I was suspicious. He must do because it could only be he who had organized the burglary of the house.

We couldn't use this information because we had obtained it illegally. How could we obtain information legally that perhaps we could use? I had asked Alice to write to AIM and she was going to give me a copy of the reply. Could I get others to do the same? Purdy would be suspicious if he suddenly got a dozen similar letters from a dozen people querying the management of their money, but maybe that was a good idea. We wanted to rattle him and make him realise that people were getting suspicious. He then might make a mistake and give us information that we needed. Or he might even stop his whole scheme, realising that it was getting dangerous. That he was close to getting discovered.

I called Pierre in the afternoon to see how he was getting on. He was on target and hoped to have some results for us the next day. We discussed the idea of trying to contact some of the people on the list and getting them to email the company with requests for information. We'd go for about twenty and see what happened when twenty emails hit Purdy's desk on Monday morning.

Pierre, excitable Frenchman that he was, was all for it. I could almost hear him rubbing his hands with glee at the end of the phone. I was a little bit more reluctant but eventually agreed that I would get on the phone that afternoon and see if I could organize something.

Looking at the list I selected twenty names who, by their profiles, seemed to me the type of people who could be persuaded. It took a few hours but, by pretending to be a fellow investor who was a bit concerned, I managed to rustle up fourteen people who agreed to send suitable emails that evening. The only reason my target was reduced to fourteen was because I found that six people either did not have computers or, if they did, they didn't know how to use emails. I wasn't going to do a training course over the phone so I kept it to fourteen. I was sure that would be enough to achieve the effect we wanted.

The effect it did achieve turned out to be considerably more dramatic than we had envisaged.

Chapter 12

The next day, Tuesday, Mike and Sophie turned up for coffee mid-morning. Sophie was full of praise for the Scottish countryside and Mike was like the proverbial cat who had found a dish of cream.

We were able to sit outside and enjoy the warm morning sun. Sophie was bubbling, full of praise for what she had seen and keen to go hiking off into the mountains as soon as she could get the opportunity.

After a while we had exhausted the tourist guide to the Trossachs and Mike asked how things were on the AIM front. Sophie came back down to earth and listened while I explained to them the results of my examination of the files. They were both as horrified and indignant is I had been.

"Bob, we've got to do something about this guy," said Mike. "There is no way he should be allowed to get away with a scam like that."

"Sure," I replied, "But don't forget we can't use any of this stuff because it would get Sophie into trouble. Hacking in to their systems is a criminal offence. You don't want her behind bars, do you?"

I then told them what Pierre and I had agreed. I showed them the list of the fourteen people who were prepared to send emails to AIM and explained our reasoning. Mike liked the idea of stirring things up. Sophie was a little more reticent, wondering what it might lead to. After all, Purdy had already shown he was capable of burglary. How much further was he capable of going?

I was able to rustle up a satisfactory lunch and Pierre arrived just as we were finishing. He had brought Sophie's laptop over and we set it up.

"Here's what I've found," he said, as he brought up on screen a list of the investments that had been made by each of the three funds.

"I've been able to identify all purchases and sales during the year. It's what you would expect. This fund has been going in and out of various stocks and bonds, presumably programming their positions to sell automatically when any investment hits a predetermined growth figure. They've even dabbled a bit in foreign exchange. The net result of all this can be seen at the bottom."

He pointed to a figure at the top of his list.

"This is the value at the beginning of the year. And this…"

He moved the cursor down to the bottom.

"… is the value at the end of the year. I've checked some of these values with records from the internet and they are correct. What it says is that this particular fund increased in value over the year by eight point two per cent, which is close to the industry average."

I powered up my computer and checked the details of the returns AIM had announced to its investors for the same fund. They had credited their investors at various rates, depending on the infamous "comments" column, at rates of between three point four per cent and five point eight. The weighted average, bearing in mind that not everybody had invested the same amount, was three point nine per cent.

"Mon Dieu," said Sophie, so shocked that she had slipped back into her mother tongue. "Cela fait plus de deux millions!"

Mike tapped her gently on the shoulder.

"Translation, please."

"Oh, sorry. That makes more than two million pounds."

"Wow."

We then ran a check on the other two funds. AIM had sold their investors short to the tune of four point eight million pounds.

There were a few moments of silence in the room while we all tried to absorb the enormity of what was going on.

I broke the silence. "This needs a bit of thinking about. This is not just a case of someone cooking the books or fiddling their expenses. This is theft on a massive scale. I suggest we reflect for a couple of days and each of us come up with a proposal as to what we should do about it. And don't forget we can't use this information without getting arrested ourselves."

I got up to pace the room and ease my back which was acting up from so much sitting.

At that point the phone rang.

It was Doug, asking if Mike was around.

I handed him the receiver. He listened attentively for a while then asked Doug if he was now back in Edinburgh.

"OK." he said. "Call here tomorrow night and update Bob. I won't be contactable," and hung up.

He turned towards us with a thoughtful look. He was starting to look concerned.

"Doug has just informed me that the villa in Spain that our friend Dewar went to for the weekend is registered in the name of a Margaret Buchanan."

"Who's she?" we asked.

Milking the mystery for effect, he went on.

"Doug has come back to Edinburgh. He didn't get the same flight as Dewar, who flew back on Sunday night, because he didn't want to risk any chance that Dewar would notice him. He flew back this morning and, anticipating that we would want to know who she was, he went hunting and, lo and behold, Margaret Buchanan is none other than ..."

Sophie broke in.

"Mrs Dewar's maiden name."

Mike looked hurt. "How did you guess?"

"Female intuition, darling," she said and gave him a hug and a kiss on the cheek."You'd better get used to it."

Mike glanced over at me with a look of resignation. Pierre and I shared a laugh at his expense, but he really didn't seem to mind.

"So this man Dewar is a close buddy of Purdy. They play squash together twice a week and he goes off, presumably regularly, to Spain where he has bought a villa worth several million pounds and registered it in the name of his wife. Sounds like a typical bent French politician," said Pierre. "And could it be that the money has somehow come from Purdy?"

He left the question hanging in the air — then went on.

"Perhaps he knows about Purdy's girlfriend and is blackmailing him."

"Or he knows about the scam and is taking a cut," I added. "One or the other would seem to fit."

"Right," said Pierre. "Let's add that into our reflections and we'll get together tomorrow and decide on the next steps."

"Not tomorrow," said Mike. "I'm afraid we can't." He looked at Sophie and took a step towards her. He put a protective arm around her shoulder and announced to us that they were going off for a couple of days — if nobody had any objections.

I pretended to look astonished. Pierre laughed. Sophie blushed and Mike looked combative. I joined in the laughter with Pierre, and Sophie demanded to know what was so funny.

"I'll tell you when you get back," I said. "Just make sure you take a camera."

There was definitely very little brotherly love in the look I got from Mike.

"Are you planning to pop in and see Heather?" I asked innocently.

Mike's response was to pick up his jacket and say to Sophie, "Come on. It's time to go before these two old farts really get started."

The next evening I heard from Doug. He had been continuing to keep an eye on Dewar and had picked up his trail at the squash club where he had known he had his regular court booked with Purdy.

"All I can tell you Bob, is that they had their game and a drink afterwards. I was able to watch them without being able to hear their conversation but there was definitely something fairly serious being discussed. It looked as if Purdy was telling him something important. Dewar was listening most of the time and when they left they gave the impression that they had come to some kind of a decision."

"Thanks, Doug," I said. "Can you switch your attention back to Purdy now for a couple of days?"

The Thursday morning sun woke me the next day. I had been fairly late in getting to sleep the previous night with my mind trying to sort out all the news we had learned from the day before.

What we knew for sure was that Purdy was skimming off millions through AIM. That he had a mistress whom he presumably wished to keep secret. That Dewar was clearly a friend of some sort and he had a villa in the south of Spain worth a lot more than he could afford on an MP's salary and he wanted to keep it quiet because he had registered it in his wife's name – no paper trail to him.

The question was whether Dewar had got the money from Purdy and whether it was because he was blackmailing him over the mistress or the fraud that he was running at AIM.

It didn't really matter which. The fundamental question was whether Dewar's money was coming from Purdy or not.

Then there was the conversation that Doug had observed. I had to consider the fact that, perhaps, Purdy had told Dewar that we were sniffing around AIM. He would have received the emails I had organized and had probably linked them to my question at the conference. Perhaps he had told Dewar of the burglary he had organized to get Alice's papers.

The scenario seemed perfectly possible but at the moment it was only supposition.

Letham is a small village. It's really not much more than a hamlet. The main street has houses down one side and stretches up to crossroads at the top. The other side is simply fields, giving a clear view across the Howe to the Lomond Hills about six miles away. There is a school and a post office and about sixty houses. It is quiet and suits me admirably. My cottage, unlike most of the others, has two storeys and is built in large chunks of granite. Half way up the street there is a lane which leads off to the right, past the village bowling green, which sits just behind my garden, and then on up to the farm. My house sits just on the corner.

Almost all the houses are set back from the road, each with its twenty feet of front garden, separated from the road, in most cases, by a low stone wall.

The owners of a good few of the houses have widened their front gates and covered the little bit of garden with gravel and park their cars there. I haven't. I like the idea of a small piece of cultivation between myself and the road and religiously look after the few rose bushes that make the house much more welcoming. There is little traffic so it is no problem to leave my car in the road. It's quite safe. One day I'll get around to building a garage up the lane at the back of the house but that is for the future.

After I had wandered up to the post office to get some milk and exchanged a few words with Mrs McLachlan about the weather I returned home to do what I had asked the others to do – think about the next steps.

I noticed that Pierre had left Sophie's laptop in the sitting room from yesterday and thought I might as well return it to him. We could have a chat about things while the young ones were probably doing their own planning. I smiled at the thought of Mike being finally hooked. Heather would be pleased.

I took the laptop and went out to the car to go off to Fernie when I suddenly remembered that I had forgotten to lock the back door. The computer was in a solid protective carrying case so I simply threw it onto the back seat and turned back to the house. I had just opened the door when the blast ripped through the air.

My front door flew back, ripped out of my hand, and crashed open against the inside wall. The explosion of hot air threw me into the house after it. I was flung onto the bottom few steps of my staircase. The unexpectedness of it left me in shock for a moment or two. I struggled to my hands and knees and turned round. My car was not a car anymore. It was a burning mess. Flames were consuming the body work furiously and black smoke was billowing up into the sky.

Once I had ascertained that I was, in fact, unhurt I got gingerly to my feet.

"Good God," I thought "What the hell was that?"

I vaguely registered the fact that I had been bloody lucky. The wall, even although it was low, must have helped to deflect the force of the explosion so that I had not been caught in the full blast. But how had it happened?

It didn't take too long to eliminate the possibility of some kind of accidental electrical fault. I hadn't even switched on the ignition. All I had done was to open the door and chuck the laptop onto the back seat and slam the door closed.

That left the only possibility. A bomb.

The noise of the explosion had brought the neighbours out. Mrs Clark came rushing out, wearing her baking apron, her hands covered in flour. Everybody was clearly shocked. Not wanting to frighten people unnecessarily I let them bandy their theories around to explain how such a strange accident could happen. I wasn't going to put forward my theory of a bomb, but undoubtedly that was what it had been.

There was no way the car could be saved but Jack, from two houses up, managed to get a hose speedily rigged up so that we could douse the flames as quickly as possible while his wife, Sally, kept on shouting at him not to get too close in case it blew up again. How it could possibly blow up twice was beyond my imagination. After about half an hour the wreck was reduced to a pile of twisted metal emitting the odd hiss as drips of water met molten steel, lost the battle and were immediately converted into a puff of steam which rose up into the air, mixing itself with the black smoke. The stench of burning rubber added to the hellish scene.

I had remained quite calm throughout the whole circus but when the crowd had dispersed and I went back inside to sit down I suddenly realised I was shaking. Delayed shock I thought to myself and sat down with a stiff whisky to calm myself down.

I was sure it had been a bomb and, if that was the case, I must have been the target. Not funny. I needed a second whisky and also someone with whom to talk it through.

I called Pierre and caught him at the hotel.

I asked him to get over as soon as he could. My voice must have sounded urgent because he didn't even ask why.

"Give me ten minutes," he said, and, sure enough, he rolled up ten minutes later. He parked up the side road, well away from the wreck, and came slowly round to the front door, a look of total consternation on his face.

He stopped short of the still-smouldering mess of burnt- out steel, his hands on his hips and slowly turned to look at me.

I said nothing but signaled him to come into the house. He dutifully followed me in and accepted the glass I thrust into his hand.

"Somebody, I think, just tried to kill me," I announced.

Pierre doesn't voice unnecessary comments. He simply sat down and took a sip of my best Bruichladdich.

"Are you serious?"

"I'm sure."

"Purdy?"

"Who else?"

"Shit!"

It was the only explanation. He must have been completely destabilised by the emails. He must have linked them to me. He knew where I lived because he had orgainsed the burglary. He had decided I was getting too close to discovering his misdeeds. Had they found out about the hacking and backtracked to Sophie's computer? I remembered Sophie telling me it was possible and she had done her hacking via my internet connection.

Pierre listened thoughtfully while I voiced my thoughts.

"There is another possibility."

"What?"

"How was it set off? It could only have been done by some kind of device which would be tripped off when you got in – which can't be the case because you're still here – or, if it was ultra-sensitive, it went off when you threw in Sophie's laptop."

He paused.

"Or it was set off by someone who was watching and it was the computer that was the target and not you."

I thought for a second.

"True, but I don't think it makes a lot of difference. The guy has definitely overstepped the mark. We're going to pull him in."

"What do you mean?"

"I've been thinking while I was waiting for you to come over. Either he tried to kill me or he tried to destroy the computer and, therefore, any evidence against him. Whichever doesn't matter – he needs to be stopped and I can think of only one way of doing it. The police are going to be no help especially as we'd have to tell them about our hacking job."

"We'll need Mike, Mac and Doug. Here's what we'll do."

I explained and Pierre's face lit up.

"I like it. But we'll have to wait until Mike and Sophie get back. We can wait a few days. If we do nothing Purdy will think he's got us off his back and be less on his guard."

Chapter 13

Mike and Sophie had arrived back the night before. When he called from Forfar I told him about the car bomb. His reaction was immediate.

"We'll be right over."

He and Sophie arrived within the hour. Both were staggered at the scene of the car. It now looked a very sorry mess of blackened twisted metal. Sophie was very solicitous of my welfare and insisted that I rerun what had happened.

We explained to them how we couldn't be sure that it was murder they had been attempting or simply the elimination of Sophie's computer.

"Well I don't suppose we'll ever know but it seems to me like the former. Surely Purdy would have realised that we would have made copies of the information."

"I suppose so," I replied. "But it doesn't really matter now. Whichever it was it's one step too far and, as far as Pierre and I are concerned, we are going to act."

I then explained to them both what we envisaged. Mike was all for it. Sophie a little less so but, as she couldn't come up with a better alternative, she went along with us. She had no part to play in the plan but was clearly concerned that we might be opening ourselves up to some unforeseen consequences.

"We'll use one of the barns at my place," suggested Mike.

Pierre hadn't visited Mike's place yet but I agreed that it would be ideal.

"Pierre and I will come up on Friday evening. Can you put us up?"

Before Mike had a chance to open his mouth, Sophie jumped in "Sure, we can," she said. Suddenly her hand went up to her mouth, she looked round at Mike, colouring slightly, "er ... can't we?"

This little byplay loosened off the tension completely. Mike leant over and put his hand on her thigh affectionately.

"Not much doubt about things now, is there? Of course they can."

Mike agreed to give his instructions to Mac and Doug and organise their side of the plan.

It was stage managed to frighten him. I wanted him scared because I needed him to crack and own up to what he had done. We couldn't prosecute. We couldn't use the information we had but we could bluff him. If I couldn't put this man behind bars then, at least I wanted him out of action and, if possible, the damage repaired.

We chose the scruffiest of the barns. The two small windows on one wall were filthy, covered with cobwebs, letting in very little light. From the beams of the roof hung a single sixty-watt light bulb giving off just enough light to illuminate the centre of the floor area, leaving the corners in shadow. Around the wall was a variety of old farm implements – old sacks, dusty boxes, an old wooden ladder, a wheel barrow, bits of wood.

I had arranged a big old table at the edge of the lit area behind which we three would sit and I placed a worm-eaten, rickety old wooden chair right in the middle about twenty feet in front of it.

We took our places behind the table and indicated to Mac to bring Purdy in. He went out to return shortly with

Doug. They had Purdy firmly clasped by the forearms and plumped him unceremoniously onto the chair facing us. Both Mac and Doug were dressed in army fatigues and had their heads covered in black woollen helmets, leaving only their eyes showing. Purdy's head was enveloped in a dirty old pillow case. His clothes were grubby and disheveled and he was trembling – the antithesis of the smooth confident smiling executive I had first met at the business conference.

I glanced sideways at Mike who was sitting on my left.

"Well you said you wanted him scared," he whispered, with a wicked grin.

I nodded to Doug who whipped off the pillow case and a totally mystified Alan Purdy blinked, shook his head a couple of times and looked around him at the miserable décor in which he found himself.

He then looked at the three of us ranged behind the table in front of him and the pile of documents in front of me. He could see and recognize me clearly as I was within the circle of light. Mike and Pierre were sitting back in the shadow. He could see there were two people but couldn't see who.

Mike told me afterwards how they had kidnapped him. Mac had an old van that he used for his painting jobs and they had simply parked it in the car park of the squash club. As luck would have it Purdy had left alone after his game and there had been nobody around. It had been very simple to grab him and throw him in the back of the van amongst the ladders and paints. Doug had sat with him keeping him quiet during the journey up to Forfar. Both had played their part perfectly. Not a word during the whole operation. Silence is a great frightener.

They had stashed him in the old cow byre, shackled to an iron ring in the wall with only the floor to sit on. He had had no idea where he was. Doug and Mac had guarded him from outside, peering occasionally in the window, which must have been exceedingly disconcerting to say the least. They had left him a couple of bottles of water and a Mars bar, but that was all.

Now here he was sitting in front of what could only be called a kangaroo court. I'd have been scared stiff.

Not perceiving any immediate physical danger, he visibly pulled himself together. He opened his mouth to speak but I cut him short before he could utter any kind of protest.

"Mr Purdy, I think you know who I am. In fact I know you do, bearing in mind that we crossed swords at your conference a couple of weeks ago and last week you organized a burglary at my home."

"I know who you are," he spat at me. "But I don't know by what right you think you can go snatching people off the street, keep them prisoner and then force them to sit through whatever farce it is you're planning."

He was angry and indignant – but still a long way from the point where I wanted him.

"I shall answer that question briefly but I will not enter into a debate on it. First, legally we have no right to do what we are doing. I will accord you that. However, we have decided to take the law into our own hands to correct a situation which the authorities have so far not been able or willing to do anything about."

He blustered and spluttered, "I demand that you let me go immediately. I shall be contacting the police as soon as possible and I'll make damned sure that you regret this. You'll be behind bars before you know where you are. All three of you."

He tried to get up but Mac and Doug thrust him, none too gently, back onto his chair.

"I don't think so. I don't think you would dare go near the police. Before you utter another word I would like to inform you that I have here in front of me documentation which, if the authorities had it in their possession, would very likely result in you spending a considerable part of the next years of your life at, as they say, Her Majesty's pleasure. You won't dare go to the police."

A part of me was rather enjoying this.

He glowered at me, his confidence still not yet deflated. "Bullshit."

I looked him straight in the eye, quietly picked up the first document, which consisted of three pages stapled together, and held it up in front of me. I pulled out my reading glasses and slowly put them on.

He didn't utter a sound but his face started to show slight signs of concern.

"Do you know a Mrs Alice Rutherford?"

"Never heard of her."

That's strange. She told us she has met you several times."

"Never heard of her."

"I have a letter here on Ailsa Investment Management notepaper addressed to this lady. It refers to several meetings with her and is signed 'yours sincerely, Alan Purdy, Chairman and Managing Director.'"

"I meet hundreds of people in my job. How do you expect me to remember them all?"

"And Mr James MacPhail?" I asked, picking up a second document.

"Who is he?"

"You wrote to him on the fourth of September last year."

He denied knowing any of the next three people I mentioned, each of whom had received letters personally signed by him.

I left a silence hanging in the air waiting until he was the one to break it. I didn't have to wait long. He must have started to realise that he wasn't in any physical danger and seemed to take hope from that. His voice almost took on its natural tone.

"Look, what's all this about? What the hell do you think you're doing kidnapping me and interrogating me as if I was a criminal?"

I didn't vouch any reply.

Mike and Pierre were still sitting in the shadow. Seen from Purdy's position it must have been very unnerving. Two hooded men in battle fatigues on either side of him. Two men in the shadows whom he couldn't make out. A stern interrogator in front of him whom he did know and who had clearly been intent on investigating his fraudulent operations. All of this in the dingiest of settings. I didn't envy him one bit. And I didn't have any sympathy for him either. When I thought of the money he had stolen and the types of people who were his prey I warmed to my task.

We sat and coldly watched a man who had systematically robbed a few hundred people just for pure financial gain. Or perhaps not. Perhaps the power his position gave him was the food that nourished the complete disregard he had exhibited towards his victims.

Pierre had lost money but he could afford it. The others had put their trust and lifetime savings into his hands, bamboozled by the inviting publicity, the dishonest marketing and the sweet talk. They had each been taken in by the image of the all-successful businessman and had lost thousands.

When we had started to probe and he saw that there was danger, ego had kidnapped his reason and he had slipped over the edge into criminal activity to protect his ill-gotten gains and his status.

"Mr Purdy, do you deny that you have embezzled important sums of money from hundreds of people who entrusted their money to your care?"

He looked up at us, as if astonished.

"You're damn right I do."

Here we had in front of us a perfect example of the much-vaunted modern financial services industry. A man of no morals who had realised that the technological advances that have made life nowadays so complicated for the average person had opened up all kinds of new ways for crime – or financial theft – in ways that were becoming more and more difficult to detect.

I couldn't help thinking that the criminal of yesterday who wanted to steal money had had to knock an old man off his bicycle and steal his wallet, or personally go into a bank or a post office and threaten everyone to get at the money in the safe. Whilst I in no way condone such behaviour at least they had had to have a certain degree of courage to acquire their loot. Nowadays they can hide behind a computer screen, miles away, or even in another continent, and steal in almost perfect tranquility, while munching a packet of crisps and sipping a cup of coffee.

"Mr Purdy, we have estimated that you have stolen from the gentleman here on my right approximately two hundred thousand pounds. You have also stolen several million pounds from most of the investors in the AIM funds. These documents that I have in front me can prove this if you don't agree with us.

"Thanks to your rapacious conduct you have made yourself an exceedingly wealthy man. We know. We have access to your computer systems."

"Hacking into a company's computer systems is a criminal offence," he barked at me. "I'll have you jailed."

"Shut up and listen to what he has to say, you little piece

of shit," said Mike, his voice coming out of the shadows. I could feel Mike was barely able to contain himself from going over and knocking the hell out of him.

I picked up the top sheet of paper from the pile in front of me.

"Alan Vesty, invested £80,000, ex-banker, sixty-nine years old. There is a commentary box here at the bottom in which it says 'Careful'.

I picked up another one at random from the pile.

"Keith Dalgleish, invested £150,000, ex-sales director, seventy-four years old. In the commentary box it says 'Went into retirement home in 2007, no known relatives, no problem'.

"Next one, 'Ethel Neale, invested £180,000, eighty years old, diagnosed with Alzheimer's in 2009, no problem'.

"'David Stevenson, seventy-six years old, invested £90,000, No knowledge, treat as normal.'"

I looked up at him. His face had lost all colour. He was visibly shocked and starting to sweat. He was frantically looking around for some means of escape. He certainly didn't want to sit there and listen to a litany of his crimes.

"Do I need to go on?"

I leant forward and picked up another piece of paper from the second pile on the table.

"This document details the investments made by AIM over the last three years with the dividends and the capital gains that were realised. The medium risk fund has averaged a return of nine per cent. You have passed on to your investors only three point nine per cent. You must have realised when I asked that question at the conference that you were in danger. You then organized a burglary at my house to steal the papers that Alice Rutherford had given me."

He was really under pressure now. He tried again to get up but Mac and Doug held him fast.

"You can't use that stuff. There's no way you can prove anything," he cried desperately.

"We are quite happy to hand ourselves in – with all of this – if you do not do what we want." I waved my hand over all the documents lying on the table in front of me. "I don't think a jury would convict. We have done nothing for personal gain - only to unmask an enormous fraud."

"You're bluffing."

"Try us. We will give you five minutes to reflect on the position you're in and then we'll tell you what we want. Put his hood back on lads and keep an eye on him."

Once he was blind again we got up and went outside, leaving him to think. A strangled cry of "You bastards!" followed us out.

Chapter 14

We went back inside five minutes later. I moved the table and chairs slightly forward so that both Pierre and Mike would now be visible to him. I then asked Mac to take off his hood.

Purdy was suddenly faced by the three of us – no one any longer in the shadows. By now all the bluster had gone. He didn't dare call our bluff. He didn't know who Mike was but he recognized Pierre immediately. "Pierre Collard! What are you doing here?" he gasped.

Pierre, in his quiet and neat way, leant forward and rested his forearms on the table and in a quiet but steely voice said,

"Mr Purdy, I don't like being screwed. I want you to compensate me for the money you have stolen from me. I calculate it to be about two hundred thousand pounds. I also want you to pay my two friends here the sum of fifty thousand pounds each as a management fee for the hard work that they have put in to get to the bottom of all this."

He gasped. "You're crazy. I can't afford that."

"Yes you can. We know, to the nearest million, how much you have stashed away in the Cayman Islands."

That stopped him in his tracks. There was a pause while he absorbed how much we knew.

"And if I do, will you then let me go?"

He must have hoped for a moment that he might get off reasonably lightly.

Plant one idea and the next one is more likely to succeed, Pierre had said beforehand. If you hit him with everything at once we might not get away with it.

"We shall see," said Pierre. "I'm not finished yet."

Purdy started to look exceedingly nervous.

"You will also transfer into a trust fund, whose trustees will be the three of us here, the sum of five million pounds for the benefit of all those who have been systematically defrauded by you. You will also sign a letter of resignation from all your positions in the Ailsa Investment Management group."

"You must be out of your minds," he screamed. "There's no way I can afford that."

"That is rubbish," said Pierre. "We know how much you have stashed away and we know that you will still have a few hundred thousand left to enjoy your retirement."

In fact we knew he would still have about a million left but we wanted him to think we had missed something. We wanted him to think that he was one up on us. That way we were more likely to win. This guy had an ego as big as a house and that would help him to accept our proposal. If we had gone for too much he might have blocked and taken the risk of calling our bluff. And what we were asking for did cover the amounts we knew he had stolen.

In the silence that followed you could almost hear his brain churning. He stared at us for about thirty seconds then all the bluster went out of him. His shoulders sagged.

"And if I agree ...?"

I could sense a slight lessening of tension behind his puffy, bloodshot eyes.

"Do it first, then we will see."

Pierre had pulled out his laptop and he fired it up.

"It can all be done here and now."

"You bastards! I don't have a choice, do I?"

"No."

He got up and walked unsteadily over to the table. Pierre vacated his seat and stood behind him while he logged on to the various sites necessary to effect the transactions. We had prepared a list of bank account numbers for the various deposits.

I produced the resignation letter for him to sign and the trust deeds which had been prepared in advance. Mike witnessed his signature. While this was going on I went next door to the WiFi printer that we had set up and brought back paper confirmations of all the transfers for him to sign. I put them carefully in a large brown envelope and, along with the other documents, placed them in my briefcase.

"Will you now let me go?" he asked, getting up from the table.

"Please sit back down in the chair over there. There are a couple of further things we would like to ask you."

Doug and Mac stood guard again.

"In addition to theft on a grand scale you have also demonstrated that you have been capable of attempted murder and we do not wish to run the risk that you might try again," I said coldly.

If he thought he was going to get away as lightly as that after what he had done to us, he had another think coming.

"What?" exploded out from the back of his throat.

"You planted a bomb in my car last week. Fortunately it exploded while I was far enough away for it not to do me any harm. However it was clearly an act of attempted murder."

"There was no intention to harm you. And anyway what proof do you have that it was me?"

In fact I had no proof. To the three of us it was obvious that it was Purdy – if not him personally, then someone acting on his orders. We were all watching him carefully. His eyes flicked from Pierre to Mike to myself and back again. Our faces were impassive and without pity. He seemed to be trying to come to some kind of a decision. His head dropped and he stared at the floor just in front of his feet. Finally, after a good thirty seconds, while nobody moved nor said anything, he looked up at us, defeat written across his features. He took a deep breath.

He must have weighed up the situation from all angles. He had admitted, although not in so many words, the scam he had been running. We had extorted reparations from him. He must have come to the conclusion that if he could convince us that there had been no intent to kill me that would be his best chance of getting out.

In a dull and defeated voice he said, "I organised the burglary which did you no harm whatsoever. I needed to get those papers to find out how much you might know. That I admit. As far as your car is concerned, it was not my idea. I was told to get rid of you. I planted the bomb in the car. Yes, that's true. But I set it off by remote control when I was sure that you wouldn't be hurt. Scared, yes, but not hurt. I could see from further up the hill. I can even tell you exactly what happened. You came out of the house, opened the rear door and threw what looked like a computer bag into the back seat and slammed the door shut. Then you went back towards your house. I suppose you must have forgotten something. I set it off when you were just opening the door. I admit I was happy to scare you but there was no way I was going to commit murder."

He looked at us pleadingly. "You've got to believe me."

The three of us looked at each other, puzzled.

"Who?" I asked coldly. "Who told you to get rid of me?"

"I can't tell you."

"Who?" roared Mike.

He flinched and turned his head towards Mike. "Look, I don't know who the hell you are but there is no way I'm going to tell you. It's not worth it. You don't know what's going on. You've found me out. Be satisfied with that and let me go."

He was almost begging.

We tried verbal bullying, softer persuasion techniques, promises, everything for at least twenty minutes but we could not get him to budge. Clearly he was far more frightened of the consequences of telling us than whatever he thought that we were capable of. Even that, in itself, made my flesh creep. Who could be capable of scaring this guy as much as that and why?

I made a sign to Mike and Pierre for us to go outside for a minute.

We all agreed that it was useless to try any more. We weren't going to get any further without resorting to some kind of torture and we weren't going to go that far.

Pierre suggested we let him go and put Mac and Doug on his tail. Perhaps we would find out that way.

We went back inside and sat down again.

"Mr Purdy, we are going to let you go. Unfortunately not immediately as you can well imagine. You will be kept here until these transfers have taken place and the AIM board has received your letter of resignation. You will then be set free and, if you want any advice from me, I would get out of the country as soon as you can. There is no way I can prevent news of your actions getting out. When the investors hear about the trust fund and your resignation is announced you can be sure there will be speculation. I personally don't ever want to see you again."

We got up and Pierre and I left. Mike stayed behind to give Doug and Mac their instructions. Purdy sat still in the chair like a broken doll.

Mike came out a few minutes later and told us he would hold Purdy until Pierre phoned to tell him when he could be set free.

"I'll give him a bit of food and when the time comes I'll have him driven back to Edinburgh and dumped near the squash club car park and he can find his own way home."

Pierre and I drove back to Fife thoughtfully. We now had another villain behind this one and he sounded like a real nasty piece of work. If he had ordered my assassination, there must be a reason and when he found out I was still alive it would be sensible to take a few precautions. The critical issue was to identify him.

We decided it would be safer for me not to go home so we booked me in at Fernie Castle. On the drive back we didn't say much. The success of our plan to unmask Purdy and obtain reparations should have been a cause for celebrations, but this was overshadowed by the news that we, or I, had another enemy who was seemingly much more dangerous.

The next morning, while the brawn of the partnership was looking after Purdy, the brains, Pierre and myself, sat down to breakfast.

"Sleep well?"

I looked up from buttering my toast and answered ruefully, "Not really. It's a bit scary knowing that someone has tried to kill you – and might well try again."

"Or might not. Whoever it is might not need to anymore."

"What do you mean?"

"Well, the danger occurred while you were trying to unmask Purdy. If that's now been done and we've put a stop to his operation we've no real reason to go on digging so perhaps he'll feel safe and back off."

"I wouldn't be sure about that. Who do you think it is?"

Pierre replied, "I was thinking about that all last night. The only people we know about who seem to have regular contact with him is the Dewar guy with his house in Spain and the lawyer that he lunches with regularly."

"So we watch Dewar closely over the next few days?"

"That's what I think, and maybe you could see if you could find out a little more about the lawyer through your golfing friend, Keith?"

Mac and Doug would not be available to watch Dewar until we had released Purdy. I could wander along to the club and see if I bumped into Keith. Meanwhile Pierre had to check up on the transfers. I thought it might also be a good idea to give Steven a tip off about possible news coming out of AIM in the very near future.

As it was Sunday we couldn't do much about the banking side of things, neither could we do anything else.

Purdy, when released, had only two alternatives. He could report back to whoever the man was that he was so frightened of or simply pack his bags and run to whatever country he chose to disappear to. But as we were not going to be able to release him before Tuesday we thought that it was unlikely that there would be any danger until then. We could relax.

We phoned Mike. Sophie answered and assured us that all was well at their end.

"Come on," I said to Pierre. "Let's go and have a round on another of our famous Fife courses."

"Fine by me," said Pierre.

So we tried to forget everything and drove down to Elie, had lunch in the Ship Inn overlooking the harbour and did battle over the local eighteen holes. I lost four and three and decided it was time I changed my clubs.

If I remember correctly from my physics classes fifty-five years ago there is some kind of principle that says that when you undertake an action there is always a reaction.

I was soon to find out the truth behind that basic law.

Chapter 15

Monday morning.

Mrs Clark came round to check that I was alright. She was still shattered by the car explosion but fortunately no damage had been done to her house. She hadn't seen me for a few days, she said, but had done some baking for me. She produced a fruit cake and a dozen scones which I dutifully accepted.

Today Pierre would be following up on the bank transfers. We had already set up the trust fund in advance, enabling us to supply a bank account for Purdy's transfer.

We couldn't release Doug or Mac yet to let them get back to Edinburgh to latch onto Dewar's tail. But, hopefully, if all the transfers went through today, we could get Purdy off our back and get moving.

I decided to follow up on Pierre's suggestion of talking to Keith about Gavin Reid, so I set off for Ladybank to see if he was around. I didn't have any other way of contacting him but he was there fairly regularly. There were few people around. When I asked the pro if he had seen Keith he told me that he hadn't seen him today but he knew he had booked a round for tomorrow. As I had made the journey over I thought I might as well get some benefit from it. I went out and had a nice quiet nine holes on my own, playing two balls whenever there was nobody on the hole behind me.

Pierre called me in the evening to confirm that all the transfers had gone through. He was back in pocket. Mike and I were now fifty grand better off. One thing I hadn't thought of was how to explain that to the tax man, but I would worry about that later.

He had also had Purdy's resignation letter delivered to AIM. I wondered how they were going to react to that. I phoned Steven and informed him that if he went round to AIM he might get a scoop.

All that was left to do was to work out how to inform all the AIM investors about the trust fund that had been set up specially to distribute some "unexpected dividends" that had accrued to them. We had all their names and addresses so it would be a question of writing a suitable letter and organising to get it mailed out. There was no real rush but I suggested to Pierre that we could work on it tomorrow morning if he came round about ten.

So the next day Pierre and I sat down to draft a circular letter to the eight hundred or so investors in the three funds of AIM. We had to come up with a policy which would be equitable to all concerned and then think up a way of explaining this bonus.

We no longer had the use of Sophie's high-speed, high-capacity laptop so Pierre had gone off to buy a new one, which would save us a lot of time compared with trying to do the job on my old steam-driven one.

It took him no time at all to fix it up. I was astonished at the power and speed of the thing.

We started by creating three lists of all the names we had, the amount they had invested and the revenue that had accrued to them over the last three years. All the information was on the back-up discs that we had. Once we had totalled up the amount distributed and compared it to the revenue that AIM had generated we had a difference of about six million. We allowed a certain amount for a reasonable percentage to AIM for their overheads and profit and got the figure down to a little over the five million.

We had to make an arbitrary decision as to how much of the five million should go to each of the three funds. That done, we could add this to the total that had been paid out and come up with a new total, which we could express as a percentage of the invested capital. As each person had received varying dividends according to the various notes in the 'commentary' box, they would be allocated the difference between the new standard percentage and the one they had received.

It sounds complicated but by using a spreadsheet the job was done fairly quickly. After a couple of hours we had three lists with an amount against each name. On average it amounted to between five and six thousand pounds for each person. They were all going to get a very pleasant surprise.

Then came the drafting of the letter.

"I'll do that tomorrow," I told Pierre because I felt we needed a break. Also I had to go round to the golf course as I knew that Keith was due to tee off at ten past two.

"Why don't you come?" I suggested to Pierre. He was more than willing. We decided to have lunch round there.

While we were halfway through our lunch Keith and Jack came in. I invited them to join us. Not wanting to have to explain the intimate details of Dad's past I introduced Pierre as a golfing friend over from France for a couple of weeks.

Keith was immediately interested and started to quiz Pierre about the supermarket industry in France. Pierre was able to describe to him how things had developed over the last thirty years and how they were now all over the place.

"Practically every town of any size has a Carrefour or a Leclerc or one of the others on the outskirts of town and, because of that, multiple stores have grown up around them. France has much more land than over here and the planning rules are not so strict, I don't think."

"I'll bet they're not," said Keith. "That's the biggest problem we have. All the bloody zone restrictions on buildable land drives me nuts. The consumers want supermarkets because we can offer cheaper prices and I'm blocked by local authorities who complain about us destroying the High Street. All I'm doing is trying to give the consumers what they want."

"They've got a point though, haven't they?" I said mildly.

"If they want to keep the wee shops in the High Street then they should give them subsidies or cut back the rates or find some other incentive. Where are the people going to park?" Keith was starting to get excited so I switched the conversation over to the upcoming Ryder Cup. I didn't want him getting apoplectic.

Keith looked at his watch.

"Tee off in fifteen minute, Jack. Would you guys like to join us?"

"Why not," I said, "Are you up for it Pierre?

It was decided and we went off to get our clubs and made our way over to the first tee.

It was sunny and warm, with just enough wind to make the game interesting. The fairways had been recently cut and the heather had not yet reached its full season's growth. Getting out of the rough was going to be easier than it would be later on in the season.

Four drives, reasonably straight down the middle and Keith was waddling off after his ball in his usual aggressive manner – short bandy legs, feet splayed out at ninety degrees and shoulders hunched. His relationship with a golf ball was definitely unhealthy. For him the ball was the enemy and he was going to make damn sure it behaved itself and did what he wanted it to do. It never occurred to him that it was an inanimate object and was only reacting to the way he hit it.

In spite of Keith's battle with the ball we had a good round and Pierre and I managed to win on the eighteenth.

Back to the bar for a beer. Jack had to leave fairly quickly and Pierre excused himself at the same time.

This was my opportunity to have a word with Keith. I suggested another drink and asked him if he had ten minutes to spare – there was something I wanted to ask him.

"Sure," he replied."How can I help you?"

"You know Gavin Reid, don't you? Wasn't he the guy you introduced to me here a few weeks ago?"

Keith looked at me warily. "Yes," he said. "Lawyer from Edinburgh. I use him from time to time. What about him?"

"Is he any good?"

"I've had no problem with him. Why? Have you heard something?"

"Oh, no. it's just that I have a friend who needs a lawyer in Edinburgh and he asked me if I knew anyone."

"What's it to do with?" asked Keith.

"I don't really know the details," I said. "Something to do with investments and finance."

"If that's what you want Reid's not the right guy. He's much more of a specialist in property deals. But I'll ask around for you if you want. I've got quite a lot of contacts over there."

"That would be great," I said. "There's no rush but if you can get me a recommendation it would be much appreciated."

We finished our drinks, took leave of each other and I drove back to Letham.

I got back to the house. I parked the hired car I had taken to replace my old Rover, which was now a jumble of burnt out metal. Must get it taken away, I thought but I had to wait for the insurance people to send in their report. It was already a week late. With the insurance money and the management fee I had extracted from Purdy I suddenly realised I could treat myself to something a bit more fitting for my station in life. That's what I would do. As soon as I got the ok from the insurance company I'd treat myself to a bright red convertible Mercedes.

With that decided I called Mike. All was in hand. They had transported a very subdued Purdy back to Edinburgh and left him outside the car park of the squash club. I wondered how he had managed to explain his absence to his wife. Well that wasn't my problem. I hoped I'd seen the last of him. Doug and Mac were now taking turns to watch Dewar.

Dad was still smiling at me from the wall as I went through to the kitchen to fix myself a coffee. I sat down to flick through the newspapers. The usual hyped-up nonsense about the goings on of some celebrity football player was splattered across the front page. Any intelligent comments on issues of note were hard to find. There was a short article on Alex Salmond's latest pronouncement on independence for Scotland. That brought me back to our man Dewar again who was, if I remembered correctly, now an SNP member.

Pierre and I had discussed who the man might be that Purdy had been too afraid of to mention. We had come to the tentative conclusion that the arrows seemed to be pointing Dewar's way. I wondered what Alex Salmond would feel about one of his members being at the bottom of a murder plot. I recalled what Pierre had said. Now that the Purdy fiasco was over and if that was the source of Dewar's extra cash, then perhaps he might back off and leave me alone.

But I wasn't at all sure and hoped that the boys were keeping a close eye on him.

The phone rang about nine thirty the next morning. I cursed, got up and went downstairs to answer it. It was Mike.

"Guess what," he said triumphantly. "It was worth our while to watch Dewar."

"What do you mean?" I asked nervously. I was starting to feel a bit uncomfortable whenever that man's name was mentioned.

"Our friend Alan Purdy has not yet flown off to the Caribbean or wherever we hope he disappears to. After we dropped him late yesterday afternoon he didn't go straight to his car and drive home as you might have thought he would."

"What did he do then?" I asked.

"In spite of the messy state he was in he went straight into the squash club, and presumably made a phone call because half an hour later Mr Bill Dewar drove up in a rather excited state and disappeared inside. Mac was watching at the time and, as neither of them had ever seen him before, he had the sense to go in and see what might be going on. They were both in the corner of the bar having a very heated discussion. Purdy was apparently ranting and raving, trying to tell Dewar something. Mac says that Dewar looked as if he was going to blow a gasket.

"They argued for about ten minutes then Purdy got up and stormed off. Doug picked him up outside and said that he drove straight home."

"And Dewar?"

"He stayed for another five minutes or so and then he left as well. He was not looking a happy man according to Mac."

"Did he go home?"

"Presumably. It was quite late. We don't actually know for sure because Mac lost him. By the time Mac got back to his car Dewar had already driven off. He says he'll pick him up tomorrow from his house. He knows where he lives."

"OK. How's Sophie by the way? Why don't you both come over tomorrow afternoon? I've got a few things I need to tell that lady."

"We'll come over but you won't tell her anything," retorted Mike. "I'll tell her all she needs to know."

I sat back and thought about the news I had just heard. We hadn't anticipated that. Purdy had seemed so scared about the man who had apparently told him to get rid of me that we thought he would stay well clear of him. That maybe wasn't Purdy's smartest move. I suspected that he would definitely be wise to skip the country now, as fast as he could.

Having nothing much to do for the rest of the day I resigned myself to do the bit of gardening that I had been promising to do for a couple of weeks.

I went up and changed into old trousers, a tee shirt and a shirt, stuck on a cap and went outside to spend a couple of hours weeding. I was very soon completely engrossed in my task. Whatever part of my mind that was not being used to make decisions about what was a flower and what was a weed became occupied with thoughts about the relationship between Purdy and Dewar. What was the hold Dewar had on Purdy? Or was it the other way round? I was convinced that Dewar knew either all about the scam of AIM or the fact that Purdy had a mistress. Either of the reasons would be enough to milk hush money from him and that would explain the hold that Dewar had over him.

Suddenly I remembered something. I got up and went indoors to the work that Pierre and I had done for the trust. A quick look through the files. There it was, near the top. A name, age, eighty-two, fifty thousand pounds, ex-miner and a comment, "No problem – one son but estranged."

The name was David Dewar and his address was in Linlithgow.

Could this be Bill Dewar's father?

I went back out to continue my weeding.

Chapter 16

Waking is a strange process – or I should say "returning to consciousness".

I had thought that perhaps dreaming would become less prevalent as one aged but this is not the case.

I was being chased for some completely illogical reason in some place that was totally strange to me. I rushed into a tall building. People were looking strangely at me. I dashed for the lift and flung myself in it as soon as the door opened. I hit a button – any damn button and the lift started to move just as my attackers were running into the lobby, guns out and, for some reason, they were wearing masks.

I noticed that I had hit the button for the fourteenth floor. The lift started to accelerate, passing floor seven, eight, nine. It showed thirteen on the LED display above the door but I could feel no sense of it slowing down. It accelerated past fourteen and carried on upwards. At twenty-five it suddenly stopped and immediately proceeded to go back down again, picking up speed as it went. I started to panic as it plunged earthwards, past fourteen again. It arrived at zero and restarted its climb upwards. I was scared rigid, sweating with fear as the bloody thing went up and down several times. Nothing I could do would stop it. I hit every button I could see but it continued inexorably doing its imitation of a yoyo, getting faster and faster while I felt more and more claustrophobic.

Through the glass doors of each floor I could see faces in a kind of a blur. Faces pressed to the glass jeering. As the lift passed every floor there they were – hands, noses, chins pressed to the glass, laughing at me.

Then I woke up. I was shaking and sweating and my heart was definitely pounding, yet I had been asleep. I realised this as soon as I was aware of my real surroundings, lying on my own bed in my own house.

That had been a few weeks ago.

However, on this particular occasion, the awakening was different. It was gradual. Consciousness came to me slowly. First my brain started to operate. I lay totally still because it was telling me that something was unusual. I was not lying in my own bed in my own house. I was somewhere else but I had no idea where.

It was cold. That was the first sensation. My mind then did a quick inventory. It flicked round my body. Everything seemed to be in the right place. Feet, legs, arms, hands, head. No pain. No obvious disorders.

I was outside. That was for sure. I was lying uncomfortably and definitely not on a bed.

The whole process of coming to my senses must have only taken a split second but there is no sense of time when you crawl out into the real world.

The five senses kicked in immediately.

Touch. I was lying on my front, face resting on something uncomfortable, my right arm and hand stretched out above my head. My hand was resting on a hard, uneven surface. It felt like rock. I moved my fingers gently and this confirmed the impression.

Sight. I wasn't about to open my eyes. I don't think I wanted to see where I was.

Sound. All I could hear was the wind. I must be outside my brain told me. Then there was the sound of a seagull, cawing raucously. Was I by the sea? Perhaps, but not for sure. Seagulls do fly a long way inland in Scotland.

Taste. Nothing. My mouth was dry.

Smell. Again the smell was of the outdoors – a musty earthy smell, mixed with a slight trace of chloroform in my nostrils.

I flicked my eyes open, not daring, as yet, to move any other muscles in my body. I looked and listened. I could only see about a foot in front of my face. There was dirt and rock just in front of my eyes and some kind of foliage was obstructing my view.

Slowly I raised my head. My field of vision was limited but it was enough to observe a rolling expanse of heather and rocks with the sight of blue grey mountains in the distance.

I checked that my feet and legs were functioning. I could feel that they were there and was relieved to find that I could move them. The same with my arms and hands.

Being now more or less fully conscious, I levered myself up into a kneeling position on all fours and moved my head slowly around the horizon.

I was out in the wilds, apparently in the middle of nowhere. Was I, in fact, dreaming?

I manoeuvered myself into a sitting position for a second and, as no one or nothing seemed to be around to prevent me, I slowly clambered to my feet, completely at a loss. So far there was no sense of fear – rather one of total bewilderment.

I felt no particular pain anywhere but I seemed to ache all over. Once on my feet the effect of the wind was greatly increased and I shivered violently. I realised how cold I was. Where the hell was I? I looked around for shelter. There was none. Only shallow dips in the ground or the customary boulders that you find out on the mountains in the wilder parts of the country.

I decided to risk the cold for a minute or two on the grounds that it was more important to try and establish where I was. I stepped over to the nearest rock and sat down and did a three hundred and sixty degree survey.

I learned nothing. All I could tell was that I was somewhere high up in the mountains and there were no obvious signs of civilization. Not a house or a road of any description.

Still no fear. More curiosity. How the hell did I get here? Because here was definitely where I was.

My memory brought back the last picture I had in my mind which was of being in my garden that afternoon where I had been pruning my roses. Or was it that afternoon? I had no sense of time. Then it came back. I had been kneeling down at the edge of the flower bed, secateurs in hand, when I had suddenly been grabbed from behind. Someone had grabbed me by both ankles and a hand had seized me by the back of my neck and forced my face down into the soil.

I touched my face. It was still covered in dirt.

It had happened so quickly that there had been nothing I could do. It must have been two people. I had been completely immobilised and then a cloth covered in some chemical had been thrust over my nose and mouth. That was all I could recall.

Who and why? I would have to work that out later.

My immediately problem was to get out of these mountains and get home. I considered my position. It was not very encouraging. Even in summer, Scotland's mountains can be very dangerous places. Practically every year there were one or two people who lost their lives up here. The weather can change in an instant and it is very easy to lose all sense of orientation. The rain can come on suddenly. The wind can get up and also the mist can appear from nowhere. Hypothermia is the big danger. I knew this and reviewed the state of my belongings. I was still dressed as I had been when I had gone out into the garden. It hadn't occurred to me that I might need a survival kit just to prune the roses. This meant thin cotton trousers, ordinary shoes and a denim shirt. Not much protection if the weather turned nasty.

I checked my pockets. Not much there either, apart from a handkerchief, some loose change and piece of string that I had taken for tying up any plants that needed it. The only positive thing was that I still had my cap which would at least keep my head warm.

Ever the optimist, I got up and tried to work out which way I should go, because the only way I was going to get out of here was by walking.

Don't blunder off in any old direction I told myself. Think it out first. First work out where north was. That was easy because the sun was right in front of me low on the horizon. I looked at my watch. Eight o'clock. The sun sets in the west. Let's watch it for a while to check that it is indeed going down. Then I can determine the points of the compass.

Observing that the sun was indeed setting enabled me to establish direction but it also meant that I was probably facing a night up here. What the temperature drop would be I had no idea but with the wind and the damp it wasn't going to be funny.

In all directions I was surrounded by mountains. Great, craggy, grey forbidding chunks of rock. They look lovely on the postcards but, right then, it felt to me that I was surrounded by enormous evil monsters, implacable, immovable, laughing at me.

What could I see in the landscape that might help me? For a start there were no trees visible. A stick therefore was unlikely to be available.

Not a house in sight. No smoke on the horizon.

There were no roads or paths that I could see, which made me wonder how they had got me up here. The only thing I could think of was that they had dumped me from a helicopter. Even two strong men couldn't have lugged me up here and then wandered off.

I figured I was not likely to be more than ten miles from somewhere – but in which direction? If I picked the wrong one and had to trek for twenty miles then I knew I was going to be in trouble. There was also the problem of food and water. Maybe there was a burn but I couldn't see one.

I had to decide – and quickly. I had to get as far as I could before dark set in.

No matter which direction I chose I was going to have to do a bit of climbing. I didn't much look forward to this but I reckoned that, at least from higher up, I might be able to have a wider view.

I decided on east. The mountains looked slightly less forbidding and I'd be walking towards the rising sun. That seemed to have some kind of sense. Whichever half of Scotland I was in there was either the coast or the A9 which sliced the country in two. A maximum of twenty miles ought to see me safe. At this point I was more angry than frightened.

It wasn't going to be long before that changed.

Disaster struck after about an hour and a half of laboriously trudging through the heather. It had been slow going because I was walking carefully. The last thing I wanted was to turn an ankle and be immobilised. The sun behind me was down on the horizon by now and dusk was setting in. But far worse than that the wind had died down and an infamous Scottish mist was descending on the whole landscape. The mountain tops had disappeared and visibility was down to about fifty yards. How was I going to be sure I was progressing in a straight line? I had heard of people getting lost in the mist and ending up walking round and round in circles.

And with the mist came that damp cold which cuts right through to the bone.

I was slowly starting to realise that this mess was not going to be as easy to get out of as I had initially thought. Hunger set in. I could handle that. Thirst was also a problem. I then started to seriously curse the bastards that had done this.

I first thought it must be revenge on the part of Purdy but, thinking a bit more about it I came to the conclusion that it was unlikely to be him. He was a bully and a coward, but I doubted he would have the guts get rid of me completely. He hadn't done so with the car bomb. But the man who instilled such fear in Purdy might. Dewar? He was an unknown quantity as far as I was concerned. As far as I knew I had upset no one else to such an extent that they wanted me dead. Because clearly that was the intention. I could see the headlines.

"Man Found Dead on Mountain. Another walker has been claimed by our inhospitable mountains. When will people learn to take survival gear with them when they go walking in the Highlands?"

It would be written off as an accident and nobody would imagine that a murder had been committed. Dewar must still consider me as a danger. Purdy would have been explaining to him what had happened to him when they were observed by Mac in the squash club. Getting rid of me would make him feel quite safe.

These thoughts actually gave me added strength. I was damned if I was going to let him get away with it.

I decided that as long as I had fifty yards visibility I would carry on up towards the cleft that I had been heading for. With a bit of luck I might get up and over and who knows what might be on the other side. I had started to climb now, occasionally having to use my hands to clamber over rocks. My bad back was giving me hell. My hands were soon scratched and bleeding. My feet ached and I had developed blisters. It required tremendous willpower to keep going.

It didn't last much longer. The mist descended inexorably until soon I could see no more than twenty yards ahead. I couldn't carry on. It was too much of a risk. I was confronted with, not only the problem of direction, but also the possibility of falling off some cliff. It wouldn't need to be a massive drop to finish me off. Falling twenty feet off a rock would probably do the trick.

There was no alternative. I was going to have to stop for the night until the sun rose and burned off the mist.

With no experience of survival techniques I only had my own common sense to rely on. The key was going to be keeping warm. A cave? A small shelter under a rock face? Anything that I could find that I could somehow turn into a makeshift cocoon to protect me.

As far as I could work out the only source of warmth was the little that my own body generated. How could I harness that? When I was younger I had done a fair amount of windsurfing so I knew the principle of the wet suit. The thin film of water next to your body warms up and acts as insulation against the colder water outside the suit. Was there any way I could use this principle?

The only thing that I could have access to were stones, earth and an abundance of heather.

I found a crack in a facing of rock which would be just large enough to take me and where the ground was dry. I started to gather heather, ripping it up with my already damaged hands. I tore at it until it was in as small pieces as possible and covered the ground where I intended to sit and doze.

By ripping strands of the heather through the open buckle of my belt I managed to create a pile of tiny bits of the plant, a bit like the lavender you might find sitting in a bowl in someone's hallway. The pile grew. There was enough of the stuff around me. The exercise also kept me moving and kept my body warm. I wanted as much as I could possibly get. This was going to be my salvation, I decided. Next to my body it would help to trap air which would be kept warm by my body heat and act as insulation. I had no idea if it would work but I couldn't think of a better idea.

The pile grew slowly. My hands got more and more scratched and my anger at Dewar more and more intense.

Finally I could go on no longer. I could just make out the time on my watch. It was nearly midnight. I knew that sunrise was only five or six hours away. I hoped I could survive until then.

I managed to cut the piece of string from my pocket into four short lengths by rubbing it against a rock. I tied each of the four pieces tightly around the ankles of my trousers and the wrists of my shirt and then proceeded to stuff my insulating material into them. I quickly filled up the legs of my trousers so that they were packed tight. The shirt was more difficult. Filling up the body was relatively easy. I was then able to fill up one arm but had to give up on the second one. I guessed that it wouldn't matter too much. It was the body that I had to keep warm. I also managed to cram the remains of my magic product into my cap and thrust it firmly down on my head.

Looking a bit like a Michelin Man with a withered arm I crawled into my crack in the rock and curled up, hoping that I would manage to see the next morning.

Before I dozed off I cursed Dewar again.

Chapter 17

The coming of the dawn after my first night in the mountains gave me hope. I was still alive, if not exactly kicking.

The sky was slowly lightening in the east and I crawled out of my shelter intending to get going as soon as possible. If nothing else the movement would bring me some warmth. Walking was not going to be easy in the state I was in. My back was aching. My feet and hands were in a mess and I decided to keep my suit of heather on in case I had to try to survive another night out. If it had actually done any good or not I had no idea. It had at least occupied me and kept the blood circulating the evening before and it had, perhaps more importantly, helped to keep my mind positive.

Count your blessings, I said to myself. You're still alive.

I managed to get into a sitting position on a rock and proceeded to slowly loosen up my muscles. Hands, arms, legs were, one by one, stretched and contracted until I felt they were reasonably operational.

While I was doing this I was searching the horizon. It was still mountain after mountain. None of them had miraculously disappeared during the night. I forced myself to stick with the direction plan I had decided on last night. I would continue east in the direction of the lightening of the sky.

The next ridge seemed miles away. I observed that I had passed the night in a rock cleft at the top of a shoulder between two peaks so the first part of my journey would be either flat or descending slightly.

Progress was more of a waddle than a walk and the movement created the added problem of the scratching on my skin. I ploughed on, head down, one foot in front of the other, a glance up every ten paces to check my direction. It was the kind of hell I had never experienced before. I imagined how Napoleon's soldiers must have felt on their long disastrous march back from Moscow.

Distance can be misleading in the hills. So can horizons. You trudge up to the ridge for an hour or two only to discover that there is hidden ground for another couple of miles before you get to that peak you wanted to climb.

It can also be deceiving on the way down. I trudged on until mid-morning.

It was an enormous struggle not to give up. What was the point of carrying on? I had had a reasonably long life. Sixty-five wasn't that bad. It had been satisfying. Why not just accept it and go and see Liz? Memories flashed through my head – all jumbled up on top of each other. My eyes wanted to close. I had to force myself to keep them open, not that I could see much as my vision was starting to become blurred. My body was telling my mind that it was suffering and didn't want to go on. Why not just sit down and rest? I didn't dare. How the hell would I get up again?

I was hungry. I had a raging thirst. I worked as hard as I could to generate saliva to keep my mouth moist but that was becoming more and more difficult.

It must have been around midday, judging from the height of the sun (thank God there had been no more mist) when the ground suddenly started to fall away. Below me was a wide valley stretching across to the beginnings of the ascent to the next ridge. It looked as if I had about five miles to cross and then a horrendous climb up the other side. Heather and rocks – desolation.

That was the lowest point of my ordeal. I very nearly gave in to it all. Bugger Bill Dewar, bugger Purdy. Just chuck it in. I risked sitting down for a minute or two on a rock and tried to pluck up the courage to carry on.

It was then that I saw the flash. It was only for a second and was far away towards the foothills of the next range. Then I saw it again. But this time it seemed to be further south. And then a third time, even further over to the right.

Suddenly I was alert. There must be a road down there even if I couldn't see it. That could only have been the sun flashing off the windows of a moving vehicle. Immediately I had hope of rescue.

I sat there for another half hour, continually keeping my legs and arms moving gently so that they would not seize up.

Then I saw the same phenomenon again – something moving flashed twice.

I stood up, groaning at the pains all over my body but light-headed and more positive again. Come on, Bob. You've only got to make it down to that road and you're safe.

"Down to that road" meant three or four miles of heather on blistered feet, picking my way around great chunks of granite and being careful not to find myself in a bog. I could see two areas of bog cotton between me and my target which would have to be circumvented, probably adding another mile onto my journey.

I made it, but God knows how. It took me three hours and when I got to the road I collapsed.

I crawled on hands and knees along the grass verge until I came to a black and white post – one of these posts which help a driver to know how deep the snow is in winter. I had absolutely no idea where I was. I could be in

Ross-shire or Sutherland – anywhere in the vast landmass that makes up the Highlands.

I could at least lean against the post, sitting down facing the road. I stretched my legs out in a V in front of me. I had to pray that a vehicle of some sort would come along. I was prepared for a wait as this was a single-track road with passing places – not one which would be likely to have a lot of traffic.

I also had to hope that a driver would see me. I could wave but I certainly couldn't get up from my sitting position. I wondered about actually lying in the road to stop a car but my brain was still agile enough to tell me that such an option would be dangerous. I was only about fifty yards from a bend and a car could easily come round so fast that they might not see me and stop in time.

All I could manage was to take out my handkerchief and tie it on to the remaining piece of string that I had and throw it out onto the middle of the road. It was white. A driver should see that, I figured.

Totally exhausted, both physically and mentally I prepared to wait. I managed to stay awake for about half an hour then I dozed off.

How long I lay there, dozing, I have no idea, but when I was awakened by a hand on my shoulder it was already heading towards dusk.

"Are you alright mate?" said a soft Highland voice.

I opened my eyes to see a kindly and concerned weather-beaten face peering at me.

I tried to answer but could do no more than croak. I had had nothing to drink during my trek down off the mountain and my throat was completely dry. I could only just clutch at his hand and give him a beseeching look.

"Christ, you're in a mess," he said. "We'd better get you to some help."

I could only nod.

"Come on then, up you get. Let's get you in the car."

I could do almost nothing myself. He managed to haul me to my feet and with my legs buckling under me he dragged me to the car. He lent me against the side while he opened the rear door, keeping a hold of me in case I toppled over. I fell any old way onto the back seat. He pushed my legs in after me and closed the door. He then got behind the wheel.

"There's a hotel at the edge of the village about four miles down the road," he said as he drove off. "I know Mrs MacDonald who owns it. She'll take you in, I'm sure."

I tried to thank him but could only manage a rough rasping noise.

When we arrived getting me out of the car proved more difficult than getting me in. "Hold on a minute," he said. "I'll be back." True to his word he was back in a couple of minutes accompanied by a woman who turned out to be the aforesaid Mrs MacDonald.

She looked at me, at first with horror, and then with concern.

"Right, Jim, you take one arm and I'll get the other. We've got to get this poor man inside."

They manipulated me out of the car and lent me across the bonnet. Jim undid the strings around my ankles and did his best to get rid of all my insulation. I was vaguely aware of Mrs MacDonald undoing the front and the sleeve of my shirt for the same purpose. They then hiked me across to the front door of the hotel and inside, leaving scatterings of heather in my wake. Once inside, I was carefully lowered into an armchair in the reception area and they both stood back to look at me properly.

I hate to think what I looked like but Mrs MacDonald was up to the task. I made signs with my hands that what

I needed desperately was something to drink. I was also shivering with the cold and the shock of my ordeal.

"Jim, there's a blanket in that cupboard over there. You get it round him while I get him a cup of tea."

I did manage to convert my rasping voice into a semblance of the word "whisky" which Jim immediately understood. He nipped into the bar and came back with the life-saving nectar and helped me to take a sip, before my cup of tea arrived.

"Take your time," said Mrs MacDonald "Get your strength back. Whatever happened to you you're safe now."

I tried to smile but that was almost beyond me as well.

"Can I leave him with you, Maggie?" asked Jim. "I need to be getting back. Or is there anything more I can do?"

"Don't worry," she said. "I'll look after him. I've got no one here tonight and I'll get the doctor to him in the morning."

I tried to thank Jim by means of signs and he left. I continued to sit there taking alternate sips of whisky and tea until at last my mouth moistened up and I was more or less able to speak. During this time Maggie sat opposite me. I was now able to take her in properly. She looked about fifty. She had neat short black hair and a kind sympathetic face. Her nice comfortable-looking figure was clad in a tartan shirt and a pair of black trousers. Her whole demeanour radiated competence.

Her brown eyes smiled at me and I managed a half-hearted smile in return. I told her how sorry I was to put her to all this bother.

"It's not a problem," she said. "What you need is a bath and a good night's sleep. We'll phone the doctor tomorrow. Do you want anything to eat?"

"No thanks, but another cup of tea would be wonderful." My voice box was operating again.

"OK, don't move. I'll fix it."

While she was gone I looked around the reception area where I was sitting. It was clearly a small Highland hotel. The board behind the reception desk showed ten hooks, all with keys hanging on them. There were a couple of prints of Highland scenes on the wall, a slightly worn grey carpet, a door half-open leading off to a room where I could just make out a couple of tables and a few chairs – obviously the breakfast room. Whether the hotel ran to evening meals I couldn't tell. The reception desk had the usual display of tourist brochures and an old-fashioned bell for summoning the management. In front there was a narrow staircase. No lift.

While I finished my second cup of tea I started to realise that my nightmare was over. I was alive and well. I confess that this realisation brought tears to my eyes. No one would ever know how close to death I had been. There had been several occasions up there when I had very nearly given up. I had had to call up all my reserves to keep going and not to simply lie down, curl up in a ball and let nature take its course.

I brushed away the beginning of tears with the back of my hand. Maggie got up and came over to me and put an arm round my shoulders.

"It's alright. You're safe now. Come on let's get you up stairs."

I nodded dumbly and tried to get up.

With Maggie holding one arm and me clutching desperately at the hand rail, we managed to make it up the stairs where she piloted me into the first bedroom we came to and there was the most wonderful sight you could imagine – a large bed with a thick inviting eiderdown. There was a door in the corner through which I could see a bathroom.

"Now you're not getting into one of my beds in the state you're in," said Maggie. "Sit there a minute."

She went into the bathroom and proceeded to run a bath. The sound of the running water was music to my ears.

"Now let's get these clothes off you."

I must have looked embarrassed because she went on. "No need to worry. You won't be the first man I've seen naked and there's no way you can take a bath on your own."

She then proceeded to help me get undressed in a perfectly matter-of-fact way which quickly dispelled any sense of embarrassment. "God, look at the state of your hands – not just your hands but the rest of you," she said.

I looked down. My feet were blistered and bloody. My hands were lacerated and the rest of my body was scratched from the heather which was now strewn all over the floor.

"Come on, in you get," she said in a kindly voice. "You can tell me tomorrow what happened to you."

With her help I lowered myself gingerly into the warm water, gave a great sigh and lay back with my eyes closed. The next thing I was aware of was a pair of gentle hands carefully soaping my body. Maggie's hands glided smoothly over me rubbing in the soap.

She then let the water run out so that she could attack the rest of me which had been under the surface. She didn't miss a corner. It was the most relaxing feeling I had had in a long time. I abandoned myself to her ministrations and said nothing. I didn't move a muscle. Even "him down there" was beyond reacting.

She then turned on the shower head that was attached to the taps and, after testing the temperature, she showered the soap off me, helped me out and dabbed me dry with a large soft towel.

I did nothing, said nothing. She was totally in charge.

She helped me across to the bed and said, "Sorry I don't have any pyjamas for you but you should be warm enough."

I gratefully slid in under the covers, totally exhausted from my ordeal.

"Maggie, I don't know how to thank you."

"We'll worry about that in the morning," she said.

She looked at me kindly and thoughtfully.

"Is there anything else you need?"

"Not really," I replied. I was half propped on the pillow looking up at the ceiling. My mind was coming to terms with my escape. It was running round in circles. I knew that, despite my exhaustion, it wasn't going to be easy to get to sleep.

She was sitting down on the end of the bed. She leant forward and patted the back of my hand.

"I'll leave the door open. Just shout if you need anything."

And she got up, switched off the light and left the room.

I lay there in the dark, thanking God that I had got back to civilization and vowing revenge on bloody Bill Dewar. But it didn't take long for the effects of the warm bath, cleanliness, exhaustion and feeling safe to lull me to sleep.

Soon I was dreaming.

It was a while since I had dreamed of Liz, but somehow she was there. We were lying on a rug in a grassy field. It was a warm sunny afternoon. I was frightened and exhausted from running away from someone. Liz was smiling and holding out her arms to me. I rolled over into her arms and she pulled my face down and pressed it to her breasts. The warmth, the softness, the smell soothed away my fear. Soon I was calm and warm. I tried to murmur my appreciation.

"Shhh!" she said. "Just go to sleep. They've gone. You're safe now."

I felt her wrap me up in her body and I slid off into sleep.

Chapter 18

I was awakened the next morning by the noise of the door opening and Maggie came in bearing a tray.

"Good morning," she said breezily. "I've brought you some breakfast if you're up to it."

It took me a few minutes to register where I was. Two days ago I had been in my garden weeding the rose beds. Now I was lying in a strange bed – somewhere. Then the drastic events of the last two days came back to me. Coming to in the middle of wild mountains. My night out in the cold. My struggle back to the road.

I had been picked up by someone and brought here. This friendly woman was Maggie. She had looked after me, bathed me and put me to bed. Now she was bringing me breakfast. It was all too much.

This all flashed through my mind in a second or two. Then I recollected my dream of Liz and I lay still and smiled for a moment or two

"Maggie, where am I? I'm sorry but I haven't a clue."

She looked surprised. "You're in Lochbervie."

"And where's that?"

"It's roughly bang in the middle of the Cairngorms."

I looked blankly at her "The Cairngorms?"

"Yes."

I struggled painfully into a half sitting position and looked at her. She was standing beside the bed with a smile on her face.

"You need to eat something," she said. "I've made you

some toast and boiled you an egg. And there's orange juice and tea."

She put the tray down carefully on the bedside table and helped me to sit up properly. "Did you sleep well? How are you feeling?"

"Much better thanks," I replied. "What time is it?"

"About nine," she replied, pulling back the curtains.

Outside the window I could see that the sun had started its daily chore of lighting up the landscape and warming up the air.

"I'd better get up," I said and turned to swing my legs out of the bed. It was then that I realised I was naked. I stopped.

"You just have your breakfast and you can get up when you feel like it," said Maggie.

As I pulled the breakfast tray across onto my lap I suddenly noticed that the second pillow beside me had been disturbed. In fact the rest of the bed seemed to bear evidence of having been occupied. I looked at it with a puzzled frown and then I looked at Maggie. She showed no reaction but moved the tray gently onto my lap and left the room with a quiet smile.

My dream resurfaced. It was still clear and vivid. Or perhaps it had not been all dream. Maybe there had been some reality mixed up in there? There was no way I could be sure so I shrugged my shoulders and, realising that I was ravenous, attacked the food.

As I ate I started to think about what I was going to do next. I had to inform Mike and Pierre of my predicament. I needed to plan with them what we should do about Dewar. But first of all I had to recover. In the state I was in that might take a few days.

I got myself out of bed with a great deal of difficulty and a considerable amount of pain. I went in to the bathroom. There was a toothbrush and some toothpaste. There was soap. There was a full-length mirror. I looked at myself. I was a mess. I took in the state of my feet, my scarred hands and the scratches on my body. I also discovered, looking around, that I had no clothes. There was a large soft towelling dressing gown hanging on the back of the door. I put it on and sat down for a few minutes. Then I got up and went over and looked out of the window. Nothing but mountains in all directions.

I had no alternative but to go downstairs in the dressing gown. I picked up the tray and made my way slowly downtairs listening carefully. There seemed to be no one else around.

Maggie was in the reception area. Barefoot I made no noise coming down the stairs. I cleared my throat so as not to give her a fright and emerged into the hallway with the tray.

"That was a magnificent breakfast," I said, when she looked up.

"Good. You seem better this morning."

"Much better, thanks to you," I said. "By the way, my name is Bob. I don't think I was in a state to tell you that last night. Bob Bruce."

"Nice to meet you, Bob. Just put the tray down there. I'll take it into the kitchen in a minute."

"Maggie, could I ask you what you've done with my clothes?"

"They've all been washed and are in the dryer. They'll be dry in about half an hour."

"I feel I owe you an explanation about how I came to be brought here last night," I said.

Maggie came round from behind her desk.

"I'll tell you what," she said. "I'll take this away" indicating the tray. "Why don't you sit in there while I make us both a cup of coffee and then you can tell me all about it?"

She disappeared through a door and I went into the room she had indicated and found myself in a snug little lounge. I took the most comfortable looking armchair available and thought about what I should do now. I knew I was going to be fine, if uncomfortable for a few days. I didn't need a doctor. My scratched body was not a real problem – more an annoyance. My hands would do. The big problem was my feet. I thought it would be a while before I could do much walking and I was going to need a softer pair of shoes.

I must, however, phone someone to come and pick me up. Heather was probably nearest.

Maggie came in a few minutes later with two mugs of steaming coffee and sat down in one of the other armchairs. I looked at her. She looked as fresh as a Highland morning and was looking across at me solicitously.

"Shall I tell you my story?" I asked.

Without going into too much detail I explained how I had apparently got on the wrong side of someone who had seemingly arranged for me to be kidnapped and dumped in the mountains. I didn't bother about all the background and said that I thought the people who had done this had probably only done it to frighten me. I didn't want Maggie thinking that it had been attempted murder, even although I was sure that that was what it was.

"The first thing I have to do is inform my sister so that she can come and pick me up because I have no means of transport. She lives in Doune. How long would it take her to get here?"

Maggie reckoned it would be about two hours. "There's a phone over there you can use."

I dialled Heather's number and it was promptly answered.

"Heather, it's Bob. I have a slight problem which I wondered if you could help me with. I'm up in the Cairngorms and my car has broken down. Is there any chance you could come and pick me up?"

I didn't want to tell her the whole story over the phone. It would only worry her.

"Does it need to be today? I've got the boys. Unless I bring them too."

"No, don't do that. If you can't come today ... Let me think ..."

I looked over at Maggie who was leafing through a magazine, not wanting to pry on my conversation. The pages stopped turning.

"And you can't do tomorrow either?"

"No."

"What about the day after?"

The pages started turning again and although her head was bent down I could just discern a small smile flitting across her face.

"Fine. You need to come to the hotel in Lochbervie and I'll see you at the beginning of the afternoon. And, by the way, if Mike or Pierre calls you, tell them I'll phone them when I get back."

I put the receiver back. "That's alright, isn't it?"

"Of course," said Maggie comfortingly. "I don't have any bookings this week so you can take it easy and recover properly."

She fetched my clothes when they were dry and I was able to go up and get dressed. We found some bandages and some ointment to treat my feet and she managed to produce a much too large pair of trainers which I could get my bandaged feet into.

"They used to belong to my son," she explained, "But he left a few things behind when he went away."

That led on to her recounting to me a bit about herself. She had two sons, twenty-eight and twenty-two. One, who had joined the Merchant Navy, was at the moment somewhere on the other side of the world and the other was working down in London.

"My husband left me six years ago and went off with his new partner to Glasgow. He didn't really fit into the landscape here and, as soon as the boys left, he moved out. These things happen. The hotel was my father's and I manage to make ends meet with it even although it's a bit off the beaten track."

Over a glass of wine in the bar I told her a short version of my story – about Liz and Callum, what I had done with my life, where I now lived and the ways I passed my time.

Maggie suggested lunch so we repaired to the kitchen and found some pâté in the fridge. My hunger had come back and I needed to make up for the last two days.

"How are the feet now?" she asked. "Up to a short walk?"

"As long as it's on paths and the mist doesn't come down," I said ruefully.

We found another of her son's left behinds – an anorak that was about my size and went out by the back of the hotel, locking everything up behind us.

We managed about two miles. My feet started to ease up after fifteen minutes or so and we profited from the warm sun, the wonderful views and got back to the hotel later in the afternoon, refreshed and relaxed.

It had been as pleasant an afternoon as I had had since Liz had died. I realised what a difference female company is compared to chatting with the lads at the golf club whose only topics of conversation seem to be sport or politics. Conversation was easy with Maggie. She was starved of it up here in the hills, she told me.

"You've no idea how the locals are not really interested in anything that happens more than about fifty miles away. Talk about navel-gazing. The Highlander's breadth of interest seems to be not much further than the next mountain!"

I suppose it was inevitable. A cozy comfortable supper in the bar – Maggie found a good bottle of wine in the cellar. We both cleared away and washed up and coffee and whisky were produced. We sat in the small lounge and had our drinks. When they were finished she looked across at me.

"Bed-time?"

There was no need to say any more. I nodded. After all, why not? Maggie was a warm and loving woman and she needed love as much as anyone else. The shock of the last two days had made me vulnerable, so without a word she slipped her hand into mine and we went upstairs. I honestly felt sure that Liz would have understood.

It was quiet and gentle love-making. None of the frenzied passion of the young but a night of giving. Each of us seemed to want to give the other as much physical pleasure as possible – the joy of giving and the joy of receiving, shared in equal measure. The years of experience we had between us combined to make the music elegant and beautiful – rising and falling like a Mendelssohn symphony as opposed to a piece of hard rock.

Afterwards Maggie snuggled up to me, resting her head on my shoulder. I gently smoothed down her hair to stop it from tickling my nose.

"Thank you," she whispered softly in my ear, and her eyes closed. Her breathing fell into the steady rhythm of sleep.

I lay awake for a while staring at the ceiling and smiling. There had been no one since Liz had gone, nor had there been anyone else while she had been alive. Making love to someone else was a novel experience. It was also nice to know that I could still make someone happy, even if only for one night.

We spent the next day quietly. Maggie diligently went about her day's business. She had to go out to get some supplies so I had an hour on my own to reflect on what had happened to me and what I would do next, once I was fully back on my feet.

I decided I would foist myself on Heather for a couple of days. I didn't think she would mind. Mike and Pierre could come over to discuss next steps. I wondered whether Mike would bring Sophie. I didn't want to think about Purdy and Dewar until I was back in Doune.

Maggie made lunch and we chatted comfortably, adding, bit by bit, more flesh onto the skeleton stories of our lives that we had described the day before.

We walked for an hour in the afternoon and I dozed in the lounge while she did some catching up on the hotel's administration. There were no guests checking in that day either which suited us just fine.

Supper, a bit of television and another night just as wonderful for both of us as the night before.

As promised, Heather turned up just after lunch the next day, muttering about irresponsible brothers who didn't keep their cars properly serviced. I introduced her to Maggie, who then left us alone so that I could tell my sister the proper story.

She didn't know the story of Purdy and AIM so I had to explain it to her. I recounted it as briefly as I could – Pierre's experience with AIM, my performance at the Conference, the hacking of their systems and the proof of wrong-doing. I then came to the bit about the bomb.

"Goodness" I think was the term she used. "Do you mean you might have been killed?"

"It looked a bit like that at the time. That's why we did what we did next."

"Which was?"

When I described how we had grabbed Purdy and put him through his trial and "persuaded" him to right all the wrongs he had done she had a hard time believing it.

"And so what are you doing up here?"

I told her simply that someone had grabbed me and carted me up here and dumped me in the mountains. I had to explain that it had taken me a couple of days to get down to here and that I needed a few more days to recover. Would it be ok if I came and stayed with her until the weekend?

"Bloody hell! This Purdy man has tried to bump you off with a car bomb and then someone dumped you up in the mountains! It's incredible! You'll have to go to the police – and straight away!"

"Look, let me rest up with you for a couple of days. We'll get Pierre and Mike over and discuss it and then decide what to do. OK?"

"Well, I suppose so," she replied.

Maggie came through and offered us a cup of tea which was gratefully accepted. I told Heather how Maggie had been very good to me when I had turned up on her doorstep, but didn't go into any detail.

Heather and Maggie chatted amiably while I sat back and watched them, only half listening. Retelling the story to Heather had got my mind going in the direction of Bill bloody Dewar.

We prepared to leave. Heather thanked Maggie for looking after me.

"Don't worry, it was a pleasure."

I added my thanks and gave her a hug and a tender kiss on the forehead and got into the car. We were just about to get in the car when I remembered I was still wearing her son's trainers.

"Nearly forgot," I said, bending down to start to undo the shoe laces.

She put her hand gently on my shoulder. "Don't worry about them. You can give them back to me next time you're passing through."

Chapter 19

Heather didn't say much on the drive back to Doune. Nor did I. I was still thinking about my ordeal. I was still full of memories of the last two days with Maggie. I was also trying to decide how to get my revenge on Dewar.

I soon dozed off.

By the time we got back to the farm it was early evening. The grandchildren had been recovered by their mother and Heather, Oliver and I had the evening to ourselves.

We ate companionably around the large pine table in the kitchen. I was at last able to take a mental step back from all that had happened over the last few days. Heather's beef casserole, the wine and cheese did wonders for my well-being. Thoughts of Maggie didn't do any harm either.

During the meal I went over the whole story again to let Oliver in on the situation.

"Sounds like Pierre has brought you a bunch of trouble," was his comment. "I can understand what you've done to Purdy and I hope all these people he screwed appreciate it but you've now got this man Dewar trying to exterminate you. That is pretty serious isn't it?"

"Well, he hasn't succeeded. He won't know that yet but, even if he did, he can't possibly know where I am now. I'll just lie low for a few days, if you guys don't mind. Is it OK if I call Pierre and Mike and get them to come down tomorrow so that we can decide what we're going to do about him?"

Heather replied, "Of course it's alright, but aren't you going to go to the police?"

"We'll see. Not yet. Anyway I've got absolutely no proof against Dewar and, as for Purdy, as far as I am concerned that problem is resolved."

I made my two phone calls. I apologized that I had not been able to be in touch for the last two days but I would explain everything if they would come over to Heather's tomorrow for lunch.

Then I had another thought. It would perhaps be a good idea if Mac and Doug came as well. They'd been watching Dewar and might have some insight that would be useful. I asked Heather and suggested that we could do a barbecue and thrash out the whole thing together.

"Fine," said Heather.

"We'll be eight then," I said.

"How come eight?" she asked. "I make it seven – us two, you and Pierre and Mike and his two cowboys."

"Just cater for eight," I said and went off to phone Mike to get him to get Doug and Mac to come over as well.

The next morning was fortunately bright and sunny. The farm was a haven of peace. Well set back from the road and on a rise, we had a beautiful view in all directions. Hills to the east, mountains in the far distance to the north and the brooding edifice of Stirling Castle, erstwhile guardian of all routes north, perched on its rock – its role in Scottish history assured forever.

Oliver and I dug out the barbecue and trundled it over to the flat patch of ground at the side of the pond. The ducks didn't seem to mind. I presume they knew that they weren't going to be the object of our cooking.

Oliver soon had everything organised and the charcoal would be hot enough in half an hour. We had time to take a break and share a glass while Heather was treating the steaks with some secret recipe she had that would result in something wonderfully succulent and delicious. I had several times tried to persuade her to tell me what she did to them but, so far, she had refused to share her secret.

We had just sat down with our glasses when Heather came out of the kitchen to check that Oliver and I were doing something useful. We thought we were but she didn't and we were immediately ordered to get the table set, find enough chairs, check the heat, set up a table over there and go in and cut the bread. We looked forlornly at our glasses of wine, which remained untouched, and got up to follow instructions.

Pierre arrived a few minutes later and after greeting Heather with Gallic flourish came out to join us. I was still walking rather gingerly on my injured feet. He watched me for a moment and asked what had happened.

"Tell you later," I said, "When the others arrive."

In the middle of this hive of activity we heard two more cars drive up to the front of the house and Mike, Sophie, Mac and Doug came round the side to join us.

I sat down again and at last managed to have a drink. I looked across at Mike and grinned. "I'll leave you to do the introductions."

Sophie, Mac and Doug were introduced to Oliver who welcomed them all.

"Where's Heather?" asked Mike.

"In the kitchen."

He put his arm round Sophie. "Coming?" he asked.

"Are you guys scared of your sister, or something?" she asked with a smile.

We both nodded furiously. "Definitely." Oliver looked on with amusement.

"Come on, Mike," said Sophie and dragged him off to the kitchen door. That left five of us round the table, glasses in hand, to watch over the barbecue.

Five pairs of raised eyebrows greeted Mike when he

came back out, on his own, a few minutes later. He came over and grabbed a spare seat. "She's put her to work. Great. Now where's my drink?"

The steaks were wonderful. The salad that Sophie had prepared was pure south of France. Just eating it one was transported to the sunshine of Provence. The wine was a delight. Light conversation flowed round the table. Mac and Doug were made to feel at home and somehow, without imposing his presence at all, Oliver was the perfect host. We concentrated on enjoying the food, the company, the sunshine and the setting, while the ducks paddled around making the odd comment in that strange language of theirs.

But at some time we had to get down to some serious discussion. After all, for all we knew, Dewar might still be intent on trying to eliminate me.

The last time I had seen Pierre or spoken to Mike had been Monday and it was now Friday and they still didn't know of my hell in the mountains.

Coffee was organised and we got down to business.

I started off by telling everybody of the arrangements Pierre and I had undertaken to distribute Purdy's largesse to the investors who had been shortchanged. I then mentioned my, perhaps significant, discovery of Mr David Dewar on the investor's list.

Doug immediately offered to follow that one up to see if he really was Bill Dewar's father.

I then explained how I had been attacked in the garden and dumped somewhere up in the mountains.

"I've absolutely no recollection of how I got there. All I can remember is being in the garden, weeding the rose beds. I was attacked from behind and the next thing I knew was that I was lying in the heather in the middle of nowhere."

Oliver and Heather had already heard the story but all the others were totally shocked. Questions came flying at me from all directions.

But ...? How ...? When ...? Who ...?

I signalled to all to quieten down. "I'm back and safe and sound. No real harm's been done except my feet and hands still need a few days to recover."

I recounted how I'd got down to the road, been picked up and taken to Maggie's hotel. No other details were necessary. Heather had come up yesterday and brought me back here "And, as you can see, I'm hale and hearty."

"What we now have to do is decide what we should do about Bill bloody Dewar."

Everybody started to speak at once. Heather and Sophie were for calling in the police. Mike was for charging over and giving the bugger a going over. Mac and Doug didn't venture an opinion. They were willing to do whatever we wanted.

Pierre was thoughtful and didn't yet express himself.

"It isn't easy," I said. "Look at what we know and what we can use. This whole thing started off with our suspicion of a fraud at AIM and my stirring things up at the conference. Purdy organised a burglary at my house presumably because he was suspicious of my interest in his company and the fact that he had seen me chatting to Alice. He was scared.

"Then we managed, thanks to Sophie, to obtain proof of his scheme and we initiated the next step – getting these dozen or so people to send emails to AIM.

"Meanwhile Mac and Doug had found out about Purdy's mistress and that he was buddies with Dewar. Dewar has an expensive house in Spain that we can't imagine where he got the funds from to buy. Also it's registered in his wife's name. The only reason for that must be that he doesn't want it known that it's his."

I paused. Everybody agreed.

"Everything points to Dewar blackmailing Purdy. Either he knows he's got a mistress or he knows of the fraud through his father, if that's who David Dewar is."

I was starting to feel that I was back up in the mountains blundering about in the mist.

"Then, my car was bombed. We now know it was Purdy because he told us – but we suspected it anyway. It couldn't have been anyone else. So we grabbed Purdy and put him through his trial. I tend to believe what Purdy told us because he showed, when he was with us, that he's a pretty weak character."

Doug broke in. "I've been watching him and I agree with you. You can tell he's slimy and he's a crook – we know that – but I don't think he's got the guts to go for murder."

"So we believe his story about being ordered to get rid of me?"

Several heads nodded. Pierre was still looking thoughtful.

"When Mike released Purdy he didn't go straight home as you might expect but ran straight to Dewar. Is that right, Mac?"

"Yes."

"What kind of a conversation did it look like?"

"Well I couldn't hear what they were saying. It's a bit difficult to describe. What was sure was that Dewar arrived in a rush. So whatever was the matter he thought it was urgent. Purdy did most of the talking. It looked like he was explaining what had happened to him. Dewar didn't say much. To begin with he looked as if didn't believe what he was hearing. Then Purdy got more excited and seemed to be trying to convince him it was all true."

"How did Dewar react?"

"To begin with he just sat there and listened. Then he started to look bloody angry. My God he's got a hard face, that bastard. When Purdy was done he leant forward towards him and looked like he was giving him instructions. Like he was ordering him to do something. Purdy didn't like it one bit and shook his head. Dewar looked like he was insisting and Purdy kept shaking his head. Then he spat a few words at him and got up and stormed out."

We all tried to imagine the scene. I could imagine Purdy but, because I had never actually seen Dewar, I built a picture of him in my head. Big, bulky, stony-faced – a hard man.

"Fine," I said. "The next thing that happens is I get kidnapped in my garden, drugged and dropped in the mountains, presumably with the intention that I don't get back. It would look like an accident. Another stupid walker who didn't take the elementary precautions when he went up into the hills."

"The whole thing is unbelievable," said Heather. "Bob, you've got to go to the police."

"And what does he tell them?" asked Mike. "We can't explain the uncovering of the AIM fraud. That puts Sophie in trouble and I'm not having that."

Sophie smiled at him and put her hand on his thigh.

"And we have no proof that Dewar kidnapped Bob. They wouldn't believe us. He's an MP and, even if they did believe us, I don't know how they could go about getting proof."

There was silence for a few minutes.

Then Pierre voiced his thoughts.

"I don't think we can do anything. We've achieved what we set out to do. We've stopped Purdy's little game. It's finished. He's resigned. If that means that Dewar no longer has a source of extra cash, then that's his problem. It strikes me that he reacted instinctively and in anger. When he stops and thinks he'll realize that there's no way that Bob could make any connection between him and Purdy. Think about it from his side. I think it was a gut reaction. He just lashed out at the guy who was the cause of him losing a lucrative source of funds. He'll drop it. He'll leave Bob alone because the risk of committing cold-blooded murder would be too great."

"Oliver, what do you think?" I asked.

"From what I've heard so far I think I agree with Pierre. It's true that you can't go to the police. Why not just lie low for a while. Dewar doesn't know you've survived. You could surface in a week or so and when you do we could ask Mac to run guard. Meanwhile Doug and Mike can keep tabs on him. I agree with Pierre. I don't think there will be any more danger."

"Everybody else?"

No one disagreed. I was in favour as well and it was my life that had been in jeopardy.

"Right," said Mike. "If that's decided I'm going for an after lunch walk. Coming Sophie?"

He held out his hand to her to help her up from the chair and they went off up the track to the hills behind. We watched them go and exchanged smiles. I bent a question mark at Heather who answered "I think she's lovely. Just what he needs. It's about time he found someone he could stick with."

"Pierre, you know Sophie better than any of us. What do you think?"

"The same as I have always thought," he replied. "If I'm too old for her then I want to like whoever does get her. My half brother will do fine."

Mike and Sophie were back in half an hour. We tidied

up and relaxed in the sun for a while. Mac and Doug left and we promised we would let them know when I decided to resurface.

Then Heather got up and announced that she had to go down to check on the horses.

"Mike, Sophie, do you want to come?" I knew that Mike was scared of the beasts but seeing that Sophie was definitely keen he acquiesced and they left Pierre, Oliver and me to finish off the wine.

We watched them go over to the paddock, Heather and Sophie in close conversation and Mike looking on solicitously. There seemed to be some kind of discussion between the girls. They were too far away for us to see exactly what was going on. Heather disappeared into the stables and came out with a saddle and bridle which she proceeded to put on one of the horses. As soon as that was completed Oliver and I were astonished to see Sophie leap up into the saddle and canter off round the field, looking every inch the accomplished rider.

She wheeled round at the far end of the field and started to gallop back towards one of the practice jumps that had been set up. Oliver and I looked at each other. He knows more about horses than I do and his comment to me was "Wow, that girl can ride!".

As she galloped up to the jump she pulled on the reins to check his speed so that he would be well placed to take off. The horse responded and sailed over the jump. Sophie rose in the saddle as they went over and leant over its neck to keep the balance right and, as the horse gathered itself on landing, she was back down with a triumphant smile splitting her face. She cantered over to Heather, jumped off and handed the reins over. Mike had been watching with obvious concern on his face.

When they came back Heather and Sophie were deep in

horse talk and Mike was following despondently behind.

"Bloody hell," he said. "She never told me she could do that."

Heather offered to put up Pierre, Mike and Sophie for the night and the offer was gratefully accepted. The evening was relaxed and harmonious – a family affair.

In the meantime I had ideas of my own on how I was going to spend my time over the next few days. My transfer had gone through. Tomorrow I was going down into Stirling to buy myself a bright red Mercedes SLR convertible and do a bit of motoring.

Maybe I would return these trainers.

Chapter 20

The next morning I set off for Stirling to see if I could track down the car I wanted. I was in luck. At the second stop I found just the model I was looking for, second hand but with only ten thousand miles on the clock. It wasn't the red I had hoped for but I accepted that blue would do. A deal was struck and I drove out of the garage as happy as a sand boy.

Keen to try out my new acquisition I headed out in the direction of Loch Lomond. It was sunny so I had lowered the hood and the long straight road west gave me the chance to feel the wind in my hair and the raunchy power of the engine. I had only driven a few miles before I was completely convinced that I had made a good choice. At the roundabout at the end of the straight I turned up towards Kippen to see how it felt on the corners. She took the narrow twisty road like a dream. No problem.

I had heard that there was a well-known village delicatessen in the main street of Kippen so I pulled over in front of Berits and Brown for a coffee stop. Sitting outside, sipping my espresso in the sun, I thought to myself that life could be worse.

The shop had an interesting selection of wines so I bought half a dozen bottles on the recommendation of the owner to donate to Oliver and Heather. I loaded up the wine, bade farewell to Mr Brown and headed on towards Loch Lomond.

I was back at the farm by lunchtime and announced my

intention to go off for a couple of days to try out my new purchase.

Pierre had left to go back to Fife, Mike had gone through to help the guys in Edinburgh and, much to my surprise and delight, Heather had suggested that Sophie stay on for a few days to help her exercise the horses.

Two days of mountain air and the open road would do wonders for my spirits. I gave strict instructions to my brain to entertain no thoughts of AIM, Purdy or Dewar.

I was back in Doune on Thursday – minus the trainers.

Relaxing after lunch I noticed the Edinburgh newspaper lying on the table and started to flick through it. Not much of interest until I came to the financial page. There was an article under the headline 'AIM boss resigns.' That interested me.

It was written by Steven and it started: 'The Board of AIM has announced with regret today the resignation of its founder Alan Purdy for health reasons.'

It then went on to explain how Purdy had started up the company and made it a major player in the investment market. The Board would sorely miss him etc. etc. No real truth in their announcement but a lot of marketing speak. It went on to say that Mr Ian McLeish would take on the role of Managing Director temporarily until the Board found a suitable successor to 'drive the business forward on the path that Mr Purdy had started'!

What, however, interested me was that I knew Ian McLeish quite well. A couple of jobs back from my retirement he had been one of the partners in the firm that had been our auditors. Knowing what I knew and thinking about the trust fund we had set up I thought it wise to get in touch with him.

I immediately called AIM and asked to be put through to him.

I was greeted like an old friend and we exchanged news about what we had each been up to over the intervening years.

"So, to what do I owe the pleasure of your call, Bob?" he asked eventually.

"How are you settling in at AIM?" I asked.

"Alright so far. But it's a funny place. There's a strange atmosphere here which I didn't expect and I can't work out exactly what it is."

"I think I might be able to help you there," I said "Are you free tomorrow morning at, let's say, ten thirty?"

He sounded puzzled but I assured him that it was probably important.

"Have you bumped into a man called Firkin yet?" I asked him.

"No."

"Well, try to find a reason to speak to him and get a feel for what he does before I come. I'll bring somebody else along and explain everything to you tomorrow."

He accepted and we hung up. I then got on the phone to Pierre and told him what I'd done and asked him if he would come along with me tomorrow. We agreed that I would pick him up and we'd go through together. I assembled all the paperwork and put it, with a copy of our disk, in my briefcase.

We arrived at the offices of AIM in George Street just in time for our appointment. It was a large smoked-glass building with a fairly discreet entrance. We were informed that AIM was on the second floor and we were shown to the lift. It opened on to a reception area. A welcome desk in the corner was staffed by an attractive receptionist who welcomed us with a chirpy voice. The rest of the floor area had low settees and a couple of glass-topped tables displaying the morning's financial press and a few copies of the *Investor's Chronicle* and other erudite magazines on finance.

The obligatory five-foot high potted plant partly obscured the light from the floor-length window and you had the impression that you could be in any office building in the world. The only identification was the large poster on the wall stating "We AIM to please" which I figured was about as corny as you could get. However, the area did give the impression of successful money which I suppose was the objective.

"Mr McLeish is expecting you. Would you come this way, please?"

We followed the swaying buttocks down the corridor and were shown into what was obviously a meeting room.

"Please take a seat. Would you like some coffee?"

"Yes please," we replied and sat down.

The coffee arrived, followed shortly by a portly, balding man in his mid-fifties in shirtsleeves and braces.

"Bob, great to see you," said Ian. "Retirement looks as if it's treating you well."

I introduced Pierre. Ian looked surprised that I had brought along a Frenchman but took it in his stride and we settled down at the table, exchanging a few pleasantries.

I had enjoyed working with Ian and knew him to be a smart, efficient and, more importantly, pragmatic professional. It was this pragmatism that had induced me to come and see him. I asked him what had led to his taking on this assignment.

"Good fees for the firm and a nice change for me," he replied with a smile.

"So what brings you to see me? Your comments on the phone yesterday sounded very mysterious."

"Did you manage to talk to Firkin?" I asked him.

"Yes I did. A slightly strange fish I thought but then I've only been a couple of days on the job and the people seem a bit different from what I'm used to."

"Ian, I don't know what you've found out so far about how things are run here but I think you'll find that everything is exceedingly compartmentalized with little or no horizontal communication, everything being channelled upwards to, what was, Alan Purdy's desk and is now yours. Does that make any sense to you?"

"Actually it does. And I was a bit surprised. How do you know that?"

Having thus demonstrated that I had a reasonable insight into the company I launched into my story.

"M. Collard here is an investor in AIM. He deposited a fairly large sum of money with them a few years ago. Several weeks ago he came to me in a state of concern about his investment and asked me if I could help him."

Ian looked intrigued. "Go on," he said, settling back more comfortably in his chair. "I've a feeling this is going to take a little time."

He took out a pen, leant over and pulled a pad of paper towards him, hand poised to take notes.

"I don't know if you've had time to look in detail at the figures yet but I've come over to tell you that Alan Purdy was running a fraudulent operation here and siphoning off a whole pile of money for himself. And he admitted it to us."

Ian was now very interested. No great expressions of disbelief or astonishment. Just a nod of his head, acknowledging that he had heard and understood what I had said.

"I've brought M. Collard along so that he can confirm everything I am about to tell you."

Ian turned to Pierre, looked at him and nodded his appreciation.

I then proceeded to recount to him the sequence of events concerning our relationship with Alan Purdy – the conference, Alice and my visit to her, the burglary and how we arrived at the conclusion that we had to do something. I then confessed to our hacking into the company's systems and explained what we had found.

Ian hadn't taken any notes. He was concentrating completely on what I said and did not interrupt. He was a good listener and I was sure he was absorbing everything.

As I had brought everything with me, I opened my briefcase and pulled out all our documentation and placed them on the table in front of him.

"That is everything we have concerning the company. There are no other copies."

He glanced at them.

"Do you mind if we stop for a second?" he asked and got up to pour himself another coffee. He came slowly back to the table, his brain obviously sifting through all that it had been asked to absorb, and sat down again.

"In there is the proof of what Pierre originally suspected. Let me show you what it looks like."

I pulled out the printout of the spreadsheet of one of the funds with its incriminating list including all the commentaries against each name and showed him.

"There are copies of this on this disc," I said, handing over to him an envelope. "You can sort them into any order to get a better understanding. We sorted them by the level of paid out return and, as you can see, all the 'negative' com-mentaries are up at the top with the corresponding low return rates."

Ian perused the list from top to bottom. And then again. He placed it down on the table in front of him and looked up at us. He was not one of these guys who explode at bad news or who are overly exuberant at good news. He always managed to display an emotional even keel.

"Bob, what you're telling me is that Alan Purdy was completely illegally ripping off, let's say, less-advantaged investors and you have here the proof and you obtained this proof by hacking into the company's systems?"

"That's a fair summary – but not wholly accurate. I can't say with certainty that what he was doing was illegal. It was certainly grossly immoral. It's possible that there are clauses in the contracts concerning levels of management fees for certain types of investments or commissions needing to be paid to people who introduced investors or whatever he could hide behind. What is sure is that it was totally immoral and he personally benefitted to the tune of several millions. He admitted it."

"He admitted it?"

"Yes."

Ian's face lost its habitual neutrality. He looked astounded.

"How come he admitted it?"

"Don't ask us the details. Let's just say that Pierre and I had a conversation with him and showed him that we knew all about what he had been up to. We offered him a way out which he accepted."

"And what was that? I suppose his resignation has something to do with it?"

I looked at Pierre, who stepped in.

"Mr McLeish, I started this all off. I am an investor in AIM and I was suspicious. I asked Bob to help me find out if my suspicions were justified." Pierre stopped for a moment and took a sip of his now lukewarm coffee and then continued.

"As Bob told you, the conference, the meeting with Alice and the burglary all raised our curiosity. I happen to be a wealthy man and the fact that I was perhaps being defrauded of a few hundred thousand pounds honestly did not worry me too much. That may seem strange to you but it's true.

"So I organised the hacking into the AIM systems. I know full well it was illegal but I'm perfectly prepared to take full responsibility.

"When we saw what Purdy was doing to elderly, helpless people – look at the comments on these lists – we decided we wanted to do something about it. Bob and I discussed it at length.

"We knew that if we went to the authorities – the police or the financial regulators – it would probably take months of investigation and there was no surety that Purdy would be adequately punished. Don't forget, we couldn't produce our proof because that could put us in prison.

"So we decided to take the law into our own hands. I know it's not very fashionable nowadays but sometimes it is the right thing to do. We met with Purdy and presented him with the evidence and forced him to make reparations and to resign."

Ian was looking more and more astonished. I could understand his concern. He had just taken over the management of an important company whose chairman had just resigned. His job was to be caretaker for six months or so and hand it over to a new man. He was not going to want to be involved in anything likely to get him in trouble.

"So, what did you do?" he asked.

I took over. "Pierre, let me explain."

"As Pierre said, we had a meeting with Alan Purdy."

I wasn't about to give the lurid details of masked men, kidnapping, the collapse of Purdy and the relief he showed when he saw his escape route.

"And …?"

"He admitted wrongdoing and agreed to set up a trust fund of five million pounds to recompense the people he had defrauded and to resign from AIM."

I pulled out another file from my briefcase and pushed it across the table. He picked it up and opened it. The first document was the trust agreement, naming Pierre and me as trustees. The second was a bank statement from the Bank of Scotland showing a credit balance of five million pounds.

Ian raised his bushy grey eyebrows and looked at us both, laid the documents carefully on the table in front of him and sat back in his chair.

"I heard that Purdy's house is up for sale. Apparently he's leaving the country. Needs warmer weather for health reasons. Is that anything to do with you?"

"Perhaps – indirectly"

"So what do you propose I do now?"

"We want to transfer the management of the fund over either to you personally or to AIM to manage the correct distribution of the funds to the people that should have had it in the first place.

"I think you'll find that your auditors are bent. We don't see how Purdy could have done what he did without sweetening their fees to turn a blind eye. If that's the case you can persuade them to find a way of getting that money back into the company and out to the investors. You can threaten to get them struck off if they don't. Once that is done I suggest you change your auditors."

"Bloody hell! You're asking me to blackmail the auditors!"

"No. We're asking you to help to correct a wrong. Purdy has been punished. True, he won't spend fifteen years in jail which is where he ought to be but he's out of the way and won't dare show his face back in the UK again. He still has enough to have a reasonable retirement but nothing like what he had planned. What's the alternative? If we hadn't acted Purdy would still be screwing people left, right and centre. If we had tipped off the authorities we'd have got nowhere and the reputation of AIM would have been mud. This way you can repair the damage and clean up AIM before handing it over. You may need to tell your successor but he should see the logic. Anyway he won't have to worry because nothing will have happened on his watch."

"No, only on mine!"

"Have you got another option?" I asked.

Ian was leaning back in his chair. He crossed his hands over his ample stomach and pursed his lips, looking thoughtfully at the documents lying in front of him. There was silence for a couple of minutes.

I was myself wondering if we had been a bit naïve in thinking we could hand over the fund just like that. But it did seem better to me that AIM should manage the process. It was really their money to be distributed and it struck me as more logical that they should control the process. There must be a way they could do it and avoid all the negative publicity that would come from making the whole thing public. It must be in the interest of AIM's auditors to find a way otherwise they would be obliged to admit collusion in the whole scam.

Ian eventually stirred. "One thing for sure is that I can't keep this to myself. Some of my colleagues are going to have to know about it. And I'm going to have to understand how he managed to keep it quiet inside the company."

"My guess," I replied, "is that he divided things up into very separate functions and didn't let anyone see the whole picture. I can well imagine him managing to do that. Firkin is probably the only guy that knew anything about it. He could well be the man who fed the comments into the database. These comment boxes are not available to anybody who simply accesses the system. They are protected by a password which our expert managed to crack."

Ian's eyebrows shot up. "This expert of yours must know what he's doing."

We made no comment.

A few more minutes of silence and suddenly Ian galvanized into action. He stood up abruptly and his chair, on its five wheels, went careering off across the room.

"OK. Here's what I'll do. I'll keep all this stuff if you don't mind. I'll have to talk to the board. They are ultimately responsible and I can't clean this mess up without letting them know what has been going on. This expert of yours – would he be willing to come here to AIM for a week and do a review of our IT systems and "accidentally" discover all that you guys have already discovered? That way the information is officially inside the company and then I can explain to the Board without getting you involved. Once they are aware of the problem they're going to be shocked. I can then – say, a couple of days later – tell them of your visit which we'll say took place after our IT review and what it discovered. How's that?"

It made sense to me. I looked at Pierre. He nodded his agreement.

"Fine," said Ian. "Where is this expert of yours? Is he in Edinburgh?"

"Our expert is, in fact, a 'she'," I replied. "Her name is Sophie Lamarre and she used to work for Pierre in his IT company in France. She now operates as an independent consultant. At the moment she is staying with my sister in Doune."

"Would she be willing to do this? I'll put her up in a good hotel in Edinburgh and pay her five grand for a week's work. The objective is to generate a report that I can present to the Board which explains all this."

"Pierre, what do you think?"

He fished in his pocket for his phone and got through to Sophie straight away. They conversed in French for a few minutes which neither Ian nor I could follow. Then Pierre hung up.

"No problem," he said. "She can be here on Monday morning and she'll ask for you."

"That's settled then," replied Ian. "We'll give your Sophie a week to produce a report. I'll speak to the Board and we'll take it from there. You hold on to the trust fund documents but don't do anything yet about contacting the investors and I'll call you back in about ten days. OK?"

Business being concluded we got up to go. Ian accompanied us down to the ground floor and we took our leave. He was looking distinctly preoccupied.

Just as we were leaving I suggested to Ian that he be careful about Firkin. "I'm pretty sure he was in on the whole thing," I warned him.

Pierre and I headed back towards Waverley station to catch our train back to Ladybank where we had left the car.

As the train travelled north, over the bridge and through the countryside of Fife, I told Pierre of the trips I had made as a kid when the trains had been powered by steam. We had revelled in the tradition of lowering the window by its strap as we puffed over the bridge and dutifully throwing the coins that Dad had given us out of the window into the steel grey waters of the Forth. This was supposed to bring us good luck.

We recovered the car, I dropped Pierre off at Fernie Castle and drove back home.

I hadn't been back since being abducted from the garden and immediately went out to review the scene of the crime. Sure enough, my secateurs and kneeling mat were still there, poignant evidence of the event. I picked them up and stowed them away in the shed.

It had been about ten days since I had been home. The wreck of my car had been cleared away by the insurance people and I looked forward to a couple of days of quiet reading, comfortable in my own home, surrounded by my few, but familiar possessions.

Chapter 21

The weekend permitted me to relax and reduce the level of adrenalin that I had been running on for the last four weeks. At my age I needed it. Thirty years ago it wouldn't have been much of a problem but nowadays I was glad that I could enjoy a bit of peace and quiet.

Pierre and I had agreed that, even although I was back in circulation again, it was highly unlikely that there would be any more danger.

I had done what I thought was right. Purdy was gone. Dewar would assume I was gone too and, when he did find out that I had survived, he no longer had a reason to get rid of me because AIM was definitively in other hands now and he would just have to get used to the idea that he had lost a neat source of revenue.

We did agree, however, just to be on the safe side, that now that I was back, Mike and Doug would keep an eye on Dewar for a week or so. Mike was happy to do so as he would then be in Edinburgh while Sophie was there.

Sophie would do a good job for Ian and I would help him in any way I could if he needed it. Pierre and I could now perhaps plan that trip round Scotland that we had talked about.

On Tuesday afternoon I got a call from Ian to tell me that Sophie had arrived the day before and that he was most impressed with her. He had introduced her to all the staff and she was now hard at work.

"There is one other thing, Bob, which might interest you."

"What's that?"

"Well you told me to keep my eye on Firkin, didn't you?"

"Yes, and ...?"

"It so happens that I can't anymore. He's resigned."

"What do you mean – resigned?"

"He came in to see me this morning and explained how he had worked very closely with Purdy and, now that he had left the company, he didn't want to stay on. He regretted it but was leaving with immediate effect – he and a guy called MacLean who works with him. They both cleared off at lunchtime, which, according to their contract, they could. I just thought I'd let you know."

"What does this guy MacLean look like? Big, muscles, crew-cut?"

"Yes. Do you know him?"

"I think so – and thanks for the information."

I wished him luck and hung up.

Firkin and No Name (MacLean) had immediately resigned the day after Sophie arrived to audit their IT systems? In the back of my mind I had suspected that they were the two who had grabbed me out of my garden and, if I was right, I didn't much like the idea of them being on the loose again.

I felt I was back in a mist again, not knowing in which direction to go. The last time I had, thank God, picked the right direction. Maggie had told me afterwards that any other direction would have left me walking twice as far before I came to any civilization. This mist was pretty thick so I sat down to think it out with a good stiff whisky.

I still thought Purdy incapable of the mountain operation and I was sure it was Dewar who was behind it. If that was the case, and if Firkin and MacLean had done the kidnapping and dumping, it must have been on

Dewar's orders. Therefore they were working for him. Perhaps he had planted them in AIM to keep an eye on Purdy. That seemed to make sense.

Conclusion: warn Mike and Doug to watch out for any meeting between these two and Dewar. I phoned Mike straight away and gave him a brief description of the two. He was to let me know if he saw any meeting taking place and, if there was one, to try and get a sense of the relationship between the three.

Over the last three years I had gradually got used to being on my own. I had slid gently into a rhythm of life which I thought suited me. The last five weeks had completely upset that, but I realised that I had enjoyed it. Apart from the obvious danger I had gone through, there had been a purpose – a certain excitement. Sitting there, thinking back to my life before Pierre had knocked on my door, I realised that things had been a bit empty. Even the house felt, all of a sudden, empty. My thoughts drifted to the quieter, calmer part of the last few weeks – Maggie.

When I had gone back to return the trainers she had definitely been glad to see me – and had said so. We had spent two totally comfortable days together, happy in each other's company. We had walked in the hills. We had explored each other's histories, likes, dislikes and experiences. It had been a haven of peace without any hint of pressure or tension. On parting I think we both knew that we would see each other again.

There was a long way to go before anything more permanent might happen but already I was wondering how it would be like being a couple again. Maybe my house did need a woman in it. Liz had never lived here so there would be no ghosts.

Suddenly I wanted to make a move.

Sophie was doing her audit. Pierre had gone back to France for a couple of days. Mike was watching Dewar. There was nothing to keep me here.

I decided that I was going to do something about it. I heaved myself up from my chair, washed up my glass in the kitchen and went straight upstairs to pack a bag. Why sit being morose when I don't have to be? I said to myself. With the house safely locked up, I knocked on Mrs. Clarke's door to tell her I was going away for a few days, threw my bag into the back of the car and hit the road north.

When I arrived Maggie was as welcoming as I had hoped she would be.

Unlike the last time, there were a few guests in the hotel but that didn't matter. They were mostly hikers or elderly couples, all of whom tended to go early to bed so we had our evenings together. I did a lot of walking which did my back no end of good. The hotel had a good stock of books and I was able to do a bit of motoring around in the glens and the mountains, appreciating the breath-taking scenery and the wildness and beauty of it all.

Saturday came round all too quickly. I had promised to check in with Mike to see how Sophie's week had gone and to hear about his tracking of Dewar.

"Sophie's week went fine. Ian McLeish was very pleased and he told her he would give you a call next week to let you know the reaction of the Board."

"And Dewar?" I asked.

"Disappeared," said Mike. "Haven't seen him since Thursday, so I reckon he's gone off to Spain. I suppose he'll be back but it looks like you don't have anything to worry about anymore. And I haven't seen the two guys you told me about."

"Great. I'll be back down tomorrow and, if you want,

Sophie can take us out for a good meal on the fees she got from AIM. I think Pierre is due back tomorrow as well."

Mike agreed and we hung up.

Saturday evening there were no guests. Maggie and I had the place to ourselves. She rustled up a magnificent meal and we shared an excellent Burgundy. The night was one of gentle love-making – completely satisfying for both of us – and we drifted off to sleep in each other's arms. How great it was to be able to give pleasure to someone again, I thought as my eyelids closed, Maggie's gentle breathing ruffling the hairs on my chest as she snuggled up against me.

We were up fairly early and, after a good Sunday breakfast I volunteered to walk down to the village shop to get the Sunday paper. It was a fresh day and the cloudless sky promised a sunny morning. The sun was still low in the sky, creating strong light and shadow on the hillsides.

I picked up the newspaper, put it under my arm and strolled back up the village street to the hotel where I knew a cup of coffee would be waiting.

We sat down in the lounge and, as usual, I started with the sports section, handing the rest of the paper to Maggie. I had got as far as the first few football reports when Maggie looked up.

"Bob, have you seen this?"

"What?"

"They've found a walker's body up in the Cairngorms."

"Thank goodness that wasn't me," I said. "It could have been, if you remember."

She handed it over to me to read.

The headline read 'Man's body found in Cairngorms'. Underneath the headlines was a head and shoulders photograph of a man in his early fifties looking seriously at the camera. I started to read the article and stopped suddenly after five lines, stunned.

"Bloody hell," I cried.

"What's up? Do you know the man?" asked Maggie.

"Not personally. I've never seen him before but I know who he is."

The article read:

The body of a man was discovered yesterday by two climbers in the Cairngorms. He has been identified as Mr Bill Dewar, SNP member of the Scottish Parliament for the constituency of Leith. The climbers discovered his body around ten o'clock in the morning as they were setting off to climb the 2,800 feet Ben Corachan. They immediately alerted the mountain rescue team which confirmed that when they found the body Mr Dewar had been dead for at least twelve hours. Initial conclusions have led them to believe that he died of exposure.

It seems to have been another tragic accident due to walkers not taking the elementary precautions required when trekking in the Highlands.

Weather conditions had apparently deteriorated dramatically on Saturday night with temperatures falling below the seasonal norm and mist and cloud cover had been very low.

Mr Dewar was fifty-four years old and lived in Linlithgow. Son of a miner, Bill Dewar worked his way up the Labour Party for several years until, in 1992, he switched his allegiance to the SNP. He was known as a busy, if somewhat abrasive personality. He served on various parliamentary committees and was Chairman of the Committee for Urban Planning.

He leaves a widow and one daughter.

There was more detail of his political career but no surmising on anything other than that it had been an accident. His car had been found ten miles down the glen.

My initial reaction was one of relief. If this was the man that Purdy had been so terrified of and who had tried to get rid of me, then here was poetic justice. And also the removal of any threat to me.

I looked across at Maggie and said, "I think that this is the man that arranged for me to be dumped up in the mountains."

"How come?" she asked.

I hadn't yet told her all the details of our adventures. I had promised I would someday, when the whole thing was finished. So I gave her a rough outline about our AIM investigation and what we had found out about Bill Dewar and why I suspected he was the one who had tried to dispose of me for having scuppered his hen with the golden egg.

"Well if it was him he's got his just desserts," said Maggie, "And he can't do any more damage. Stupid idiot. He knew the dangers of the mountains. Serves him right."

I had other thoughts. I excused myself and got up. "I'm just going for a ten-minute walk. Got some thinking to do," I said and went out of the hotel and up the path that Maggie and I had taken the morning after my rescue.

She had hit the nail on the head. Dewar knew the dangers. Why would he be so daft as to go rambling in the mountains himself? It didn't make sense. What if it wasn't an accident? What if someone had got rid of Dewar using the same method that they had employed to try to get rid of me? And what if the perpetrators had also been Firkin and MacLean?

This turned my previous theory on its head. If that was the case, then Firkin and MacLean had been inserted into AIM by someone else and for another reason. But what the hell could the other reason be? Who could have wanted Dewar removed and why?

I was due to go back down to Fife today so I would leave the issue until I could discuss it with the others.

Each goodbye was becoming a little more difficult for me. I happened to say this as I was about to drive off. She only nodded and said "I know" with a sad smile. But we had agreed that she would take a break soon and come down to Letham for a few days. I promised I would call her the next day and we would try to fix a date.

I was back home by five. I showered and checked with the hotel that Pierre was back. Mike and Sophie were staying there as well so we all arranged to meet up at seven.

When I went into the bar the other three had already arrived. Pierre, as usual, was looking neat and elegant. The new Mike (same guy but looking a lot more at ease with himself) perched on a bar stool with a protective arm round Sophie's shoulders. And Sophie looking stunning in a short red shirt dress, which hugged her figure and showed off her tanned legs to perfection.

After welcomes and a quick drink we all settled down at a corner table, looking forward to partaking of whatever delights the chef could conjure up for us.

"Nice time in France then?" asked Mike.

Pierre smiled and nodded, without offering any more explanation.

"And you? Bob – where have you been?"

"Trying out the new motor for a few days," I replied. None of them knew about Maggie and I wanted it kept that way – for the moment at least.

"And you, Sophie? I hope you didn't have to work too hard for that nice fee that you're going to use for tonight's supper."

"It was fine. Basically I just redid officially what we had already done before and tarted it up for presentation to the Board. Ian seemed very pleased and said he would be calling you sometime next week to let you know what they decide to do. And Mike and I did some sightseeing – just like tourists."

We did ourselves proud as far as the meal was concerned. It was the first time for a while that we had all sat down together and it really felt like family. Mike and I looked at each other and I felt that he thought the same way. In fact his response to my glance was "Pity Heather and Oliver aren't here."

We all agreed and promised to include them the next time.

An excellent lobster bisque, a piece of Aberdeen Angus fillet, done to perfection, followed by a selection of prime cheeses – suitably accompanied by a couple of French wines chosen by Pierre and I was ready to break the news about Dewar. We ordered coffee and malts all round and I sat back and looked at this new family of mine.

"I have some news for you. If you are all at ease, I would like an opinion from each of you."

I had caught their attention.

"Pierre, you have just come back from whatever you were up to in France. Mike and Sophie have probably been staring into each other's eyes all day. But I have read today's paper. I'd like to read you an article."

I pulled out the cutting I had taken that morning and read it out to them. When I had finished it I passed it round. Everyone reread it.

"Before you say anything, I have had time to think about it and I'd like to voice my thoughts. Very simply, here's how I see it. We investigated AIM and discovered the fraud that Purdy was practising on its investors. During the process I was "warned off" by a certain Mr Firkin and his side-kick who, I have discovered, is a Mr MacLean.

"Purdy confessed, righted the wrong he had done and has cleared off. Someone then tried to get rid of me in the mountains – aided or abetted by the two men who grabbed me from my garden. Purdy also told us that someone had instructed him to bomb my car but was too scared to say whom. Then we found Dewar with more money than he should have. We thought that Dewar was blackmailing Purdy and that AIM was the source of his extra money.

"We presumed that when Dewar found out that I was responsible for cutting off his source of cash he got me dumped in the mountains for revenge.

"So far that all seemed to hang together. Although I didn't tell you this, I thought that probably Firkin and his colleague (I didn't know his name at the time) were the two who kidnapped me and that they were Dewar's inside men at AIM. Then Ian MacLeish called me last week to tell me that these two had suddenly resigned from AIM the day after Sophie started working there."

I paused for a sip of my whisky and went on.

"Now we find that Dewar is dead – supposedly an accident – from exposure in the mountains – exactly the same method that was used to, hopefully, dispose of me. For me this doesn't make sense. If Dewar chose that method to get rid of me then he must be stupid to go off and die that way himself. In other words I don't think it was an accident. I think Firkin and MacLean got rid of Dewar."

"Shit!" – that was Mike.

A thoughtful look – that was Pierre.

"Merde!" – that was Sophie.

"So my question is: If I'm right, why did someone need to get rid of Dewar? And who? Was it Firkin and MacLean themselves or were they acting for someone else?"

The first reaction was from Sophie.

"One thing is for sure. We need to find out because we need to know if Bob – or any of the rest of us – is still in danger."

Mike, instinctive as always, jumped in. "We need to track down this Firkin and MacLean and find out if they are linked to someone or if they are acting on their own. I can do that with Mac and Doug."

"To be honest, I think they are acting on orders. I've met them. Remember they were the two that took me off to a meeting after the conference. They didn't seem to me to be the type of guys who were controlling anything. They felt like subordinates."

Pierre, meanwhile, had said nothing. He was not one to blurt out his first thoughts. He was looking pensive, listening to what we had to say – clearly weighing up his own view.

I looked across at him and raised my eyebrows in a question. He shook his head slowly, a faint smile on his lips.

"Possible," he admitted. "Let's suppose that there is someone else further in the background. Then there must be other machinations going on behind which are important enough to warrant the removal of Dewar as soon as the cards started tumbling down after the disappearance of Purdy. N'est-ce pas?"

I didn't comment. It looked like the whole story wasn't over yet. Something was floating around in the back of my brain. It was some kind of half-formed thought – as if I had missed something. It was as if there was one piece of the puzzle that I needed in order to connect everything up. I felt that I knew or had seen something which was significant but I didn't know what it was, or why.

I decided to stay the night at the hotel. The wine with

the meal and the several whiskies consumed with the coffee made it sensible not to risk driving.

I left them to it, explaining that I was tired after the long drive and the excellent meal.

"See you all in the morning," I said and took myself off up to bed.

I couldn't get to sleep at first. Thoughts of Firkin and MacLean, of mist in the mountains, of Maggie were all jumbled up in my head.

Chapter 22

I awoke refreshed after a decent night's sleep in the luxury of one of the hotel's bedrooms. Showered and shaved I went down to breakfast to find Mike and Sophie in deep discussion over eggs and bacon and toast. Pierre had apparently not yet made an appearance.

Mike informed me that he had been in touch with Doug and they were both going to spend a few days in Edinburgh to try and keep an eye on our two targets. Sophie was clearly not too happy about this, sensing perhaps some danger for Mike but he reassured her that there was no problem. He and Doug could look after themselves if there was any trouble.

He asked me if I could find out an address for either of them.

"Sure," I said "I'll call Ian MacLeish. They must have some information in the personnel department."

I called him straight after breakfast and gave Mike the two addresses he had supplied. Mike had arranged for Sophie to go and stay with Heather for a couple of days where she could help with exercising the horses and he set off for the capital as soon as he could.

Pierre came down for a late breakfast after they had gone and I shared a cup of coffee with him. I brought him up to date on what Mike and Sophie were doing.

"Well, there's not much we can do for the moment," said Pierre. "What do you fancy doing over the next few days? Let's do a bit of touring. I need a guide. We'll take our clubs and go off up north. I fancy visiting a few distilleries and I'll foot the bill. After what you've been through you need a break. How about it?"

It didn't take me long to decide.

We set off that morning on the strict understanding that no discussion was allowed on the subject of Purdy, Dewar and the rest.

We drifted gently though the hills of north Fife and crossed over the Tay by the road bridge leading into Dundee. I was able to point out to Pierre the other famous Scottish railway bridge – this time a replacement of the original one which had suffered a catastrophic accident on a cold December night in 1879. During high winds, gusting up to eighty miles an hour, the bridge had collapsed while a train carrying an estimated seventy-five people was crossing. The train and a large section of the bridge disappeared into the night waters of the Tay. There were no survivors.

Travelling with Pierre was a "no expenses spared" experience. We planned to play Carnoustie the next day so we checked in for the night at the Carnoustie Golf Hotel, on the edge of the golf course and a couple of hundred yards from the beach. A bracing walk on the fine white sands preceded a relaxed meal and an early night in anticipation of doing battle with the famous links course.

We had no trouble getting a tee off time the next morning.

We went to pay our green fee and when the professional discovered that Pierre was French he looked up and winked at me.

"Wait a minute," he said and disappeared into the back office to emerge a minute later with a pair of green wellington boots which, with a deadpan face, he handed to Pierre. "You'll probably be needin' these then," he said.

Pierre, recalling the story of his famous countryman who

had lost the British Open on the last hole by trying to play out of the Barry Burn in his barefeet, took the joke well.

"No thanks," he said. "I'll make sure I lay up short."

Carnoustie is a tough challenge to anyone's golf but we got round it without disgracing ourselves and headed off the next day to Speyside. The weather was perfect. A sunny day, the occasional scudding clouds breaking the monotony of the blue heavens and painting the hills and mountains with shadows which moved across their slopes and crags so that every second the image was different. A photographer's paradise.

Glenshee, Braemar (a stop for lunch), past Balmoral and on through Tomintoul to Granton on Spey. I was much more familiar with the west coast which, as a boy, we had explored extensively, so this was new country to me and I enjoyed the discoveries as much as Pierre.

The required visits to a few of the well-known distilleries the next day resulted in us accumulating several cases of prime malt which would only just fit into the boot of the car – the back seat having to be occupied with the golf clubs. We had the rest of the cases shipped down to Fife.

I had promised Pierre two more rounds of golf so we did Nairn and Royal Dornoch to round off a week of marvellous escapism.

On the drive back down the A9 my thoughts started to turn to the Lowlands and, having put everything out of my mind for five days, I became impatient to get back in touch with Mike to find out how his week had been.

I had left him my key so when we got back to Letham mid-afternoon he and Sophie were comfortably ensconced in my living room.

We unloaded the car and Pierre handed over the case of whisky that he had bought for Mike and the (rather expensive) Celtic brooch he had bought for Sophie.

Pierre enthusiastically described our trip while I sat comfortably, thinking again how much our lives had changed since he had arrived. I glanced over at Dad's photo and winked at him. He was still smiling back at us, as if watching and approving.

Sophie cooked us a superb supper. They had been down to the coast the day before and she had gone crazy in the fish shop in Anstruther. A seafood salad was followed by sole in a sauce that she had dreamed up from whatever she could find in my kitchen. She hadn't found all she needed so had gaily gone round to Mrs Clark to borrow some herbs. My larder was raided for a dry white wine and we settled down to as good a meal as Pierre and I had had all week.

Meanwhile, while she was putting all this together, I broached the subject of Mike's week in Edinburgh.

"Not a lot to report I'm afraid. I followed Firkin and Doug took on MacLean. They just seemed to be going about normal business. A bit of shopping, quite a lot of time spent in their respective homes. They only got together twice as far as we could make out. Once was just a meeting in a pub in the High Street. The second time they met a guy who I think I've seen somewhere before but I can't remember where. I must admit I didn't like the look of him. They met him for lunch in an Italian restaurant down in Leith. As you said you wanted some idea of any relationships they might have Doug and I went in and sat well away from them, but where we could see their table."

"What did this man look like?" I asked.

"A professional type, I would say. He was a bit overweight, dressed in a suit and tie and looked about fifty, going bald and he seemed to be the one who was in control of the situation. Firkin did most of the talking.

MacLean hardly said anything and the other guy listened and asked the odd question. You got the feeling that it was a serious business meeting."

"Did he look as if he was their boss?"

"Yes," answered Mike. "He was certainly the dominant personality in the discussion."

I glanced at Pierre, "Any thoughts?"

Mike went on. "I managed to get a photo of him."

He passed over to me a slightly blurred shot that he had obviously taken in the restaurant. I recognized Firkin and MacLean and confirmed this to the other two. I was the only one of us who had met them. "That's them," I said and passed the photo to Pierre.

He looked at it for a minute.

"We've seen that other man before. Isn't he the lawyer who was at the conference and who used to have lunch with Purdy?"

"Yes, that's him. A man called Gavin Reid. We presumed he was Purdy's lawyer."

"And do you think he could be the Mr Big behind all this?" asked Mike. "I must say I didn't like the look of him. I followed him for a bit after he left and there was something I didn't like about the way he thrust himself past people as if they weren't there. As if he was above everybody. He had a kind of a supercilious look as he wandered along and he's got a weak, cruel face. I even saw him kick a cat out of the way as he was walking and he looked as if he enjoyed doing it. Do you know what I mean?"

"Yes. I've met him – briefly – once before. And then I also saw him at the conference."

"If he is the man who got Firkin and MacLean to get rid of Dewar and tried to get rid of you we'd better do something about it. All three of them are wandering around on the loose. They could do anything."

Sophie announced supper and we left the discussion to enjoy the food.

I said little during the meal and let Mike hold centre stage, regaling Sophie and Pierre with tales of Scottish history and anecdotes of his soldiering days around the world.

I enjoyed the food and the wine and thought about Gavin Reid.

During our coffee the conversation came back to Firkin, MacLean and Reid.

"I've been wondering about this lawyer, Reid." said Pierre. "He and Dewar must have known about each other. Lawyers are one of the main sources that asset management companies use for finding investors aren't they? If he and Purdy were working together – and Reid was getting his share – he had every reason to be mad at you for bringing down the house of cards. That would give him a motive for getting rid of you.

"And if Dewar was blackmailing Purdy he would know about that as well. It strikes me that Reid had every interest in Dewar disappearing as well to make sure his connection to Purdy never got out."

I was only half listening. Suddenly, while Pierre had been expounding his theory, a piece of lateral thinking had hit me.

Ideas sometimes come into one's brain sideways. I've often been aware of my capacity for lateral thinking and, if anything, I've tried to develop it. I've always let my brain drift and not keep to the straightforward route that logic tries to dictate. I had read Peter Drucker's book on the subject when I was younger and had always appreciated the value of letting one's mind roam.

Strange thing the brain. It must have been working away, without my knowledge and then brought up to the surface a message "Hey, Bob, what if ...?"

It had to do with the similarity of my adventure in the mountains and Dewar's death. Something in that newspaper article that, at the time, hadn't seemed of much significance but ...

Had I just found that elusive information that had bothered me a few nights before?

I had made a rather weird connection that, at first sight, seemed ridiculous but, the more I thought about it, and the more I thought about the characters involved, the more I started to wonder if, perhaps, I had an explanation for the whole scenario. If I was right, then things were a lot more serious than any of us had thought. And I didn't like the idea of that at all.

I didn't voice my thoughts to the others. I would sleep on it, review the issue again the next morning and then decide what to do.

Pierre was watching me.

"You look very thoughtful, Bob," he said. "Care to share with us?"

I declined. "Just thinking," I said. "Don't worry about it."

He seemed a bit put out but shrugged his shoulders and said, "OK, but if you do want to knock some ideas about, let me know."

At this stage I had no intention of voicing my theories to the three of them. If I was right we had already had two murder attempts – one of which had fortunately been unsuccessful. I didn't want any of the others exposed to a similar threat.

As I only had one spare room Pierre went back to the hotel for the night. I retired early and left a very domesticated Mike helping Sophie to do the clearing up. They seemed to have hit it off in a big way and I was happy for them both.

I retired to bed but couldn't sleep. I lay in bed and chatted in my mind to Liz and Maggie in about equal proportions. I thought again about Dad and Pierre. I then reviewed my theory concerning Gavin Reid and his two cowboys. It still seemed to make sense.

Finally, wanting to sleep, I switched my thoughts to other things. I replayed my round at Royal Dornoch. I had been hitting the ball well and had beaten Pierre three and two. I smiled to myself at the memory of the twenty-yard chip I had sunk on the sixteenth to seal the match.

Then I drifted off to sleep.

Chapter 23

The next morning I decided to follow up on my theory. Although I was still a bit unclear in my head as to exactly what the next steps should be, one thing I did know was that I needed some information and the best person to get that for me was Steven.

I got through to him straight away and explained to him what I wanted to know. He told me that he didn't know how to find that out himself but he had a friend who could probably help.

"Is this urgent, Bob?" he asked.

"Yes. And on no account mention my name."

And then he added "Is this anything to do with AIM?"

As there was no way he could have made the connection his question took me by surprise. It was so off-centre that I wondered how to reply.

"It could be," I said guardedly. "But keep it one hundred per cent confidential. I've no idea at the moment, but if anything comes of it I'll let you know and you'll have the inside on a bigger story than you think."

There were a couple of seconds of silence at the end of the phone.

"OK. I'll call you tomorrow morning. I'll make my questions as innocuous as possible and let you know what I can find out."

"Thanks, Steven," and I hung up.

Steven was as good as his word. He called me back late morning the next day.

"No problem to find out what you wanted to know,

Bob." he told me. "It's all public information. You just need to know where to look – which I didn't but my friend did."

I listened carefully to what he had to say. When he had finished I asked him the two follow-up questions that I needed an answer to.

"That would represent an investment of, roughly, how much would you say?"

"It's not exactly my area of expertise but I'd say somewhere in the region of five to ten million. I can check it out for you if you want."

"And the potential value?"

"Impossible to say but my guess is that you could, if everything worked out, multiply that by at least ten."

"Thanks, Steven. That's helped me a lot. I can't tell you any more at the moment but I promise you you'll get your story as soon as I have checked out a few other things. In the meantime forget that this phone call ever happened."

"Don't worry. I've you to thank for the inside edge about AIM and I'll say nothing. I'm off for a couple of weeks to Spain for a holiday anyway. I'll call you when I get back."

I put down the receiver, sat back and, resting my elbows on the arms of my chair, I raised my hands and put my fingertips together and let out a slow quiet whistle. That was certainly enough money to kill for, I thought to myself.

Next port of call – Keith. He knew Gavin Reid. I wondered if he was available for a game of golf.

I phoned the club house to ask David, the pro, if he had Keith's phone number. He had. As he was a busy man, running around all over Scotland in his private helicopter, I thought I would wait and try to get him in the evening.

After supper I got through to him and asked him if he was up for eighteen holes the next day.

"Hold on a minute, Bob," he replied. "Let me check."

He returned to the phone after about a minute.

"Sorry. Can't do tomorrow but I am free the day after, in the afternoon. I'd be delighted to take another twenty quid off you."

"Great," I said. "I'll book us a tee for two o'clock. How's that?"

"Fine. See you then."

Keith had just arrived when I drew into the car park. He wandered over as I got out of the car.

"Afternoon, Bob. New motor? Won the lottery have you?"

I smiled. "Not really – just a little consulting fee. I decided to treat myself."

He was his usual bustling self, eager to get to battle, and we walked over the railway to the clubhouse together. Another warm and sunny afternoon. The course was looking in superb condition and as there weren't too many people around we got off on time. Today I was determined to play some good golf and when we were finished I could talk to him quietly in the clubhouse afterwards.

I was looking forward to a good competitive round. We went at it seriously. No strokes were given or taken as Keith's handicap was only two more than mine. We shared the first few holes thanks to one long putt from Keith on the second and a miss from three feet by me on the third – one of those ones that tickled the edge of the hole, ran round the back and stayed out. I controlled my frustration as we stepped up onto the next tee. Forget it, I said to myself. You can't do anything about it now. Just concentrate on the next hole.

Keith lost the next two, we halved six and seven and he hauled one back at the eighth. Things weren't going too badly. I was driving reasonably straight, although not very long. Keith visited the rough a couple of times. We both played the ninth perfectly. As it's a slight dog-leg to the left it's a hole where the placing of the drive is important to get a decent shot at the green. Both of us were on the green in two and two putted. Two pars in front of the clubhouse is always a nice feeling so we were in good spirits as we attacked the tenth.

"Only one down and nine chances to get in front," said Keith with a wicked smile. "Come on, Bruce, let's see what you're like under pressure."

Pressure helped me control my iron shot to the par three tenth and I hit the green dead centre. Keith, attacking the ball pugnaciously, brought his hands through just a little too quickly and his shot faded off into the greenside bunker.

As we walked up the fairway he was muttering to himself, forehead furrowed and eyebrows gathered together as if to keep the sun out. I couldn't help thinking that I wouldn't like to cross him in business. There were moments when he looked as if he would be utterly ruthless in the pursuit of his goals.

All was sunshine and roses, however, a few minutes later when he played out to four feet and sunk the put to halve the hole.

The battle continued, never more than a hole apart until we got to the sixteenth tee which is right down at the bottom end of the course. The last three holes at Ladybank run alongside the drive up to the clubhouse from the main road. It's narrow with almost no room for cars to pass and is lined by beech trees on the left and denser trees and shrubs on the right as you drive up to the car park. Playing the last three holes back to the clubhouse these beech trees form a major hazard for those of us who have a tendency to slice off the tee.

The sixteenth is a dog-leg left where you have two choices – play straight, but not too strong or you're in the trees or try to cut the corner over a strategically placed bunker and a chunk of heather on the left.

I chose the former strategy and Keith the latter.

Keith didn't quite clear the corner which meant he was in the heather and I, unfortunately, connected with more than my usual effectiveness. I watched with anguish as my ball bounced once and disappeared into the trees.

We were in no particular hurry as there was no one on the hole behind. So Keith set off to look for his ball while I headed off across the fairway into the trees.

"See you on the green," I said cheerfully as I kept my eye on the spot where I had seen my ball disappear. Keeping one's eye firmly fixed on the line is the key to not losing too many golf balls. You don't look around you but walk in a straight line to the spot that you have registered. One of the first lessons Dad had given me when I was a wee lad.

But this was one occasion when I shouldn't have followed his advice.

I entered the trees, pulling my caddy car behind me and searching the ground for that pesky little white ball.

I was about ten yards into the trees when they jumped me. There were again two of them. They must have been hiding behind the trees waiting. Looking back on it I suppose that if I hadn't drifted into the trees on that hole they would have moved up to the seventeenth or the eighteenth. It didn't change much. I was grabbed from behind by a pair of very strong arms and a hand rammed a cloth against my face, drenched in some kind of chemical. I gagged. I had no chance to shout out to Keith before my head started spinning and I lost consciousness.

It was a total surprise. I had no time to think. No time

to struggle. No time to realise what had happened to me until sometime later – I had no idea if it was five minutes or fifty – I came groggily to the surface and found myself in the back of a car, blindfold, being driven to some unknown destination.

When I stirred and groaned my way into consciousness I was made aware that there was someone sitting beside me. I presume I was in the back seat. I was told roughly to shut up and keep quiet. I obeyed. There didn't seem much point in doing anything else as I couldn't move anyway. My hands and ankles were firmly bound by what felt like some kind of nylon cord.

After about ten minutes the nausea had abated and my brain started to function again.

I had recognized David Firkin's voice. I presumed that MacLean must be the driver. This didn't surprise me. What had taken me unawares, however, was the speed of reaction. Never underestimate the opposition. I had done exactly that. They had moved much faster than I had expected.

Steven's information had given me a possible motive that I imagined could, to certain people, justify getting rid of two people – me and, more importantly, Dewar. I had no doubt that Dewar's death was murder even although I had no way of proving it.

Wasn't the eternal question that the police asked themselves when trying to solve any murder "Why?"?

There had to be a motive. The reason might turn out to be strange to others but, to the perpetrator, it had to be sufficiently strong. That's where I thought Pierre's theory fell down. It didn't seem strong enough to me for murdering two people. Even if Dewar did know of Reid's involvement in AIM it just didn't seem to be enough of a reason to need to murder him.

Like a fool I had wanted to gather a bit more evidence before acting. The fact that it was starting to look as if I had been right was no comfort. I was in trouble. And because I'd kept my suspicions to myself, I couldn't rely on any outside help.

Chapter 24

A short while later I was aware that we had turned off the main road and we seemed to be travelling up a long driveway. I could hear the crunching of the gravel under the wheels and there was no longer the noise of other traffic. Although the car was travelling slowly the driveway seemed quite long until we eventually came to a halt.

The driver got out and came round to my side of the car and opened the door. He undid the cord that was around my ankles and hauled me to my feet. No loosening of the blind fold. No untying of my wrists. Without a word he took me by the upper arm and proceeded to pilot me forward.

I stumbled on a step.

"Twelve," he said tersely.

He hauled me up the twelve steps and, once again on level ground, we proceeded forwards. I could sense that we had gone through a door. I was still in my golf shoes and the noise made by my studs changed from stone to what sounded like wood and then to carpet.

We turned right. I could hear the noise of a door being opened and I was pushed through into what was, presumably, the front room of whatever this building was.

Any attempt I made at asking him what this was all about was met with total silence. Silence is not only frustrating but also very unnerving – especially if you are bound and blindfold. I tried to tell myself that perhaps I could talk myself out of this. Anything to keep the mind positive.

I could hear the noise of a chair being pulled over behind me and I was forced down into it. My legs were quickly bound to each leg of the chair and my hands were untied. I could in no way struggle. I couldn't match the strength of my captors. My hands were immediately and firmly tied to each arm so that I was completely immobile. My escort then left, having checked that I was completely secure and I heard the door close after him.

I could do nothing but sit there and wait.

I had a suspicion I knew where I was but no way of being sure. What seemed to confirm my idea was the total absence of noise.

My senses had given me the impression of a building of large spaces and, as far as the entrance and this room were concerned, sparsely furnished. Small rooms with lots of furniture absorb noise and don't give off the same echoes. And once I was alone there was total silence. No birdsong, no traffic noise in the distance. Just complete stillness.

I must have been left there for about twenty minutes but I had no way of telling. Even with vision it wouldn't have helped because I wasn't wearing a watch. I don't when I play golf. I hate the thing rattling around on my wrist.

Then the door opened and I sensed the arrival of several people. I could feel two walk past me and a third stopped just beside me. The blindfold was removed and I was able to take in the situation.

I was sitting in the middle of a fairly large room of the style you would associate with a large country house. It was on the ground floor. I was partly facing three bay windows looking out onto a lawn of some sort. In the distance were trees. It was obviously a large well-to-do property. High ceilings, tastefully wallpapered and carpeted. There was little furniture – a table against one wall with a drinks tray on it. The two arm chairs in the corner facing me were occupied by my expected acquaintances, Firkin and MacLean. They were watching me carefully. The door must be behind me.

I turned my head to take in the man standing beside me. It was indeed Gavin Reid looking much as I remembered him. Portly, balding, dressed in a two-piece suit. He had a glass of what I presumed was whisky in one hand and a cigarette in the other. He was looking down at me coldly and dispassionately.

I reacted as naturally as I could.

"What the hell is this all about?" I asked.

He looked at me for a second without replying. Then, without any change of expression other than a faint glint in his eye he took a cigarette lighter out of his pocket, flicked it on to give a healthy flame and bent down and applied it to the bottom hem of my cotton golf trousers.

"Hey!" I yelled at him. "What are you doing?"

He offered no explanation but held the flame steadily until, with horror, I realised that my trousers were starting to catch fire. The flame caught gradually and I started to feel the heat as it crept slowly upwards. I struggled and wrenched at my bonds – anything to try to avoid the pain that I knew was coming.

It didn't take long. Within seconds I could feel the scorching intensity of the flesh burning on the front of my shin. I screamed.

Reid walked slowly over to the drinks tray by the wall and picked up a soda siphon. Without any hurry he came over to me and aimed it at the burning cloth. He pressed the lever and a heaven-sent jet of soda water extinguished the flame and left me gasping for breath after the sheer hell of the burning.

I felt sick. I had burst out in a sweat. I was facing a

maniac was all I could think of. He looked down at me with an evil smile.

When the immediate relief effect of the water had disappeared I realised that my shin was badly burnt and it started to hurt like hell. This guy was a torturer – and not one of those ones who does it against their will ("This is going to hurt me more than it hurts you!") but a real sadist. A man who took pleasure from inflicting pain on others.

I yelled across at the other two, "Stop him, for God's sake!" Little reaction. They did at least have the grace to look a bit uncomfortable about it but it was clear they were not going to do anything.

I looked up at Reid who was standing in front of me, seemingly totally unperturbed.

"What the hell do you think you're doing?" I yelled at him, hauling at my bonds in the hope that I could free myself. All I achieved was more pain from grazing my wrists and ankles.

Reid walked over to the table, stubbed out his cigarette and set down his glass.

He took off his jacket and hung it carefully on the back of another chair and came over to stand in front of me – still with that evil grin on his face.

"Mr Bruce," he said "I've just given you a taste of what might happen to you if you do not cooperate with me. You have stuck your nose into affairs that should not have concerned you and you are now going to suffer the consequences. I warn you now. You are completely within my power and I can do exactly what I want to you. I admit that I enjoy inflicting pain. Always have. I don't know why but that's the way it is and you, unfortunately, find yourself in a situation where I can enjoy myself to the full."

He walked round the chair and, without warning, lashed out at the side of my face. This time the pain was momentary but the shock effect was considerable. The force was such that the chair very nearly toppled over.

"What is it that you want?" I gasped.

"I need information from you," he replied. "But not too quickly, otherwise I won't have the opportunity to have my fun."

The matter-of-fact manner that he said this filled me with dread. The burn was stinging and throbbing like crazy. My head was still ringing from the blow. I was horrified by what he might think of next. And I was right to be.

He continued talking as he prepared for his next trick. I had great difficulty in concentrating on what he was saying while I watched him.

"I would like to know why it was that you started looking into the affairs of AIM."

He was emptying things out of a large cardboard box that was lying on the floor over by the wall.

"I would like to know what you know about any connection between AIM and a certain Mr Bill Dewar."

The first thing he took out was a poker which he laid on the floor in front of me. He then took out a blowtorch which had a small canister of gas attached to it. This he also put down on the floor beside the poker.

"I would like to know why you decided to visit AIM the other day and what you discussed."

He then took out an extension electric cable and an iron which he proceeded to connect up to the socket in the wall. He placed the iron on the table. He turned to me.

"In short, I wish to know everything that you know, and I wish to be utterly convinced that everything you tell me will be the truth."

He picked up the blowtorch and lit it with his lighter. When the flame was suitably strong he picked up the poker and applied it to it.

"Are you willing to talk?"

"I don't know what you're talking about," I said desperately, hoping that there was a degree of bluff in his pantomime. "I'm prepared to discuss anything with you if you will untie me and let me up from this chair."

"I'm afraid I can't do that," he replied. "Now let's see if this is hot enough yet."

He removed the end of the poker from the flame and without any reticence whatsoever walked over to me and lowered it onto my thigh.

"Shit!" I cried out and my whole body convulsed. He took it off after only two seconds but that was enough to have burned a hole right through my trousers and leave a searing gash on my skin. It was agony. The smile turned into a leer.

"Now you've seen what the poker can do. We'll soon be passing on to the iron when it's suitably heated up."

He walked over to it and picked it up and turned the surface up towards him. He spat on it. The spittle sizzled and evaporated in seconds. "Not quite hot enough yet."

I was in one hell of a mess. The two goons in the corner were going to do nothing. I was at the mercy of a madman who should be locked up and there was nothing I could do about it.

"Look, if you let me loose I'll tell you everything I know."

"Or guess?"

"Or have guessed," I confirmed. "Just let me up and put those damned things away."

He stepped forwards and slapped me again. Once more it wasn't the pain but the shock that created the effect.

"Bruce, I'm not mucking about here. I want everything

you know or have guessed about AIM and if I don't get it fast I'm going to really go to town on you. In fact, I don't honestly think you'll survive it."

He was starting to perspire. Beads of sweat had started to appear on his forehead. His bloodshot eyes were lit up with eager anticipation of the plans he had for me. And I could do nothing.

He picked up the poker again.

"No," I screamed.

He ignored me and applied it for even longer to my other thigh. The pain was viciously intense. You couldn't call it unbearable because I bore it. I had no choice. But it seemed to notch up every nerve ending in my body. I screamed and retched. I couldn't stop myself.

Coupled to the pain this time was the smell of burning flesh. My own flesh. There was a horrific wound, black and bleeding, across the middle of my thigh, about a foot long.

When I had recovered some sanity I gazed at him, gasping for breath.

"Look, I dug into AIM's affairs because a suspicious investor asked me to. That's all. I guessed Dewar was blackmailing Purdy but I couldn't care less about that. That wasn't my business. Anyway, I read he had got himself killed up in the mountains, so I don't see what difference it makes now. And I visited AIM the other day simply to explain to them what I knew about Purdy's fraud. I don't know anything else and that's the truth."

"Let's assume that is the truth and that is all you know," said Reid, walking over to the iron and picking it up. "You still haven't told me what you might have guessed or suspected. That is very important to me."

He walked over towards me with the iron in his hand. He held it about six inches from my face. I could feel the intense heat emanating from it. Suddenly he thrust it against my arm. I wrenched myself away from it so hard that the chair fell over. With the pain and the shock I had blacked out for a few seconds. Reid dropped the iron and hauled me back up into a sitting position and left me there like a rag doll. He strolled over to the table to pour himself another glass of whisky. He took a satisfying sip and looked over at me and let out a sigh.

It was then that I heard the noise of a car on the gravel outside and steps coming into the house. The door opened and someone entered. The footsteps came over towards my chair. I couldn't turn round to see who it was but I was pretty sure I knew.

"OK , Gavin, that's enough for the moment," said a voice with its distinctive accent and a familiar figure materialised in front of me.

Chapter 25

The newcomer flashed a questioning look at Reid.

"What does he know?" he asked.

"He's only admitted to what is obvious but he hasn't yet confessed to what he might have guessed. Neither has he told us if he has talked to anyone else."

"That's what's critical. Even if he has guessed we can simply get rid of him and nobody will be any the wiser. If he has voiced his suspicions to anyone else we have a real problem on our hands."

I looked up and tried to focus on the face of the man standing in front of me – the man I had last seen on the sixteenth tee of the golf course.

He was standing in front of me glowering. He lent forward, grabbed a handful of my hair and shook my head.

"Are you listening to me, Bob? Can you hear me?" There was controlled anger in his voice. I knew this man and I knew that it wouldn't take much for him to lose that control. And he had his insane lieutenant to carry out whatever he was asked to do. I shuddered.

He took a step back and put his hands on his hips. His jaw was thrust out towards me and he proceeded to explain.

"You have got yourself in one hell of a mess and it's entirely your own fault." He practically spat the words at me.

"By sticking your nose into AIM and that petty little prick Purdy's cash machine you've mucked up a much bigger operation. That idiot Dewar, who I had eating out of my hand, panicked, with the net result that I've had to get rid of him and now I have to reconstruct something to replace him. It's going to set me back five years and I can't afford that."

His voice was getting louder. He was almost shouting. I needed to calm him down. If I could buy any time there was always hope.

"Don't know what you're talking about," I managed to mumble.

"I think you do," he said. "You may be a pretty crummy golfer, but you aren't stupid. You know that Dewar was getting paid by AIM."

I nodded, "Sure," I managed to get out. "He was blackmailing Purdy."

"Like hell he was," he retorted. "It was me who was blackmailing Purdy. And he was paying Dewar on my behalf. You maybe didn't know that at the beginning but you worked it out later, didn't you?"

It wasn't going to do me any good to deny it. I figured I might as well admit that I had worked it out and see what it was he wanted from me.

I looked at him with disgust. I discovered afterwards that McDowell's seemingly highly successful business was in severe financial trouble. He had borrowed up to the hilt and his only escape was to accelerate his growth to generate funds to reduce his debt burden. He had been on the danger of collapse and was willing to take desperate measures to survive.

I spoke slowly, trying to spin out the conversation as long as possible. I forced myself to ignore the pain in my legs and arm, which wasn't easy. They were burning like hell.

"Yes, I worked it out. Dewar held a key position in the

planning permission process and you were paying him to accelerate approvals for new supermarkets. You're sitting on about twenty chunks of land that you have accumulated over the last few years and you need planning permission pushed through to build new stores."

"You're bloody right I do," he fired back at me. "And you've buggered the whole thing up. I had to get rid of Dewar and now it'll take me years to get them through thanks to all these bloody anti-supermarket groups floating around all over the place.

"Well, I'm afraid you're going to have to pay for your stupidity."

"What do you mean?"

McDowell had walked over to the table by the wall and poured himself a whisky. He knocked it back in one gulp and slammed the glass down on the wooden surface. Reid was still standing off on one side watching. The other two hadn't stirred from their chairs.

He swung round to face me.

"Who else have you told? Who else knows? The new guy at AIM?"

Here was his problem. He could presumably rely on the other three to keep their mouths shut. If I had told nobody then he simply had to dispose of me and he was safe. If I had shared my information with anybody else he was in a mess.

"Nobody," I replied, which, unfortunately, was the truth.

"I'm afraid I don't believe you," he said. "Here's the bottom line. I need to be completely convinced that nobody else could suspect a relationship between me and Dewar and you're the only person who can do that. As far as I'm concerned the only other people who could are here in this room. So far you haven't convinced me."

I reiterated my denial. "I've told absolutely nobody. I couldn't, because until now it was only a theory. I had no proof." I tried to sound as convincing as I could. "For God's sake let me out of this chair and we can discuss this sensibly."

"No. I'm afraid you're going to have to stay there and go through a lot more pain. Once Mr Reid here is finished with you and you still stick to your story I might start to believe you. But until then, the jury's out."

I struggled again at my bonds. I yelled at him. "It won't do any good. I can't tell you something that's not true. No matter what he does the answer's always going to be the same. I've told nobody."

All I got as a reply was, "We'll see."

I collapsed back into the chair and watched with dread as he nodded at Reid and stepped back. Reid went for the poker again and the blowtorch. He picked up the blowtorch first and set it alight adjusting the flame to its fullest. He was about to bend down for the poker when the front window exploded inwards.

Not only did the window explode but Reid uttered a shriek and collapsed to the floor. All hell was let loose.

A split second after the explosion two masked figures in combat gear burst in through the window, followed a second or two later by a third.

They were fully armed. It was like a scene from a television SWAT team film. The first figure went straight for Firkin and MacLean in the corner and put them out of action with two swift blows to the head with what looked like a cosh.

The second man went straight for Keith McDowell and dropped him gasping to the ground with a thundering blow to the gut, just under the breast bone. He collapsed to the floor, retching and gasping for breath.

The third man went for Reid. But there was less need of speed in his case. He was writhing on the floor screaming. The explosion of the window must have been caused by a bullet because he was clutching his shattered right arm and there was blood all over his fingers. The blowtorch had fallen out of his hand and he had landed on top of it. The man hauled him off it to reveal his scorched shirt and chest. Reid was totally out of action trying to clutch his injured arm and his burnt chest at the same time and screaming in pain.

The whole episode must have taken no more than about ten seconds.

The three men then produced rolls of masking tape and proceeded to bind, gag and blindfold all four of their victims. There had been no speech between them. Without a word being spoken twenty seconds later my four tormentors had been totally immobilized.

I could only watch in amazement. It looked as if, against all the odds, I had been rescued. Waiting for someone to come over and cut me loose I heard the sound of the door opening and I tried to crane my neck round. I couldn't. It hurt too much.

Someone came in quickly through the door and stepped round to the front of my chair. He crouched down and looked earnestly into my face. His eyes wandered over the sorry state of my legs. "Bob, are you OK?"

It was Pierre, concern showing on his welcome face. Never had I been more relieved in my life. I nodded speechlessly.

"Listen, we've not got much time," he said quickly. "You'll be fine now. We have to leave immediately. These guys can't touch you anymore but I have to leave you as you are. The police will be here in about two minutes. We've got to get out before they arrive."

I nodded dumbly.

"I'll explain later," said Pierre. "Come on guys we've got to go."

I could hear the sound of police sirens in the distance, but approaching quickly.

"OK, off you go." I could see why they wanted to be gone before the police arrived.

The last words from Pierre were, "You don't know what happened. You don't know who rescued you. They were just three masked men. OK? If you plead total ignorance they'll never find out. See you."

And the four of them disappeared out of the window and off into the shadows of the gathering dusk.

I was left alone surrounded by four immobilized bodies who, just a few minutes before, had been intending to put me through unimaginable torture.

Two minutes later two police cars screeched to a halt in front of the house. I could see the blue flashing lights reflected against the remains of the front windows and within seconds six uniformed officers pounded into the room.

I recognised the man in charge immediately – Chief Inspector Bob Davis from St Andrews. I had played golf a couple of times with him in competitions.

He stopped, aghast at the sight in front of him.

He looked at me, the four bodies and the shattered window.

"Jesus! Bob Bruce! What the hell's been going on here?"

"If you could just cut me free I'll tell you – and I suggest you handcuff all these guys and take them into custody."

He cut me loose as quickly as he could, looking with despair at my burns. He helped me to my feet but I couldn't stand. I collapsed back into the chair.

"You need to get to the hospital as soon as possible," he

said, and called over two of his men. Before they helped me up I gave Bill a very quick explanation of what had happened, but not why.

"These two over there kidnapped me and brought me here. That one," pointing to Reid, "has been torturing me. I think he has been shot and also burned. He'll need medical care but, please, not at the same hospital as me!"

"And I think you know who that is" I added, pointing to Keith McDowell.

"I certainly do."

"Well, believe it or not he was the boss behind the whole business. He is accessory to torture and murder and I think you'll find that one of these three will give you the evidence you need. Can you hold them all overnight?"

"Sure. But who tied them all up?"

"I was rescued by three masked men in combat gear. They came in through the window, neutralised them all and then scarpered when they heard your sirens. God knows who they were but they've gone.

"Listen, could you get me to the hospital in Cupar please? And, if you come round tomorrow and I'm up to it, I'll tell you the whole story. If you want to take photos of all this before your guys take me off, go ahead. I can hang on for a few minutes."

Bill confirmed he would hold them all overnight and come and see me the next afternoon. He took photos of the scene, including my wounds and his two officers helped me out to the car and took me off to the hospital.

Chapter 26

On the car journey to hospital there was no conversation. I couldn't have talked if I tried. I surrendered to the intense relief of being safe. I could bear the pain much more easily now that I knew there would be no more and that soon it would all heal and disappear. My wounds would leave a few scars but I honestly didn't care.

The policemen arranged for me to be taken care of as soon as we arrived. My wounds were cleaned and dressed and, with a healthy dose of painkillers, I was installed in a private room and took no more than a few minutes to crash out.

I had been assured by Dr Bishan that they would all heal but that I was liable to have to stay in for four days. I hoped that the hospital bed crisis that we kept on hearing about would oblige them to let me home earlier. I managed to get one of the nurses to promise me that she would contact Fernie Castle and pass on my news to Pierre.

I awoke late the next morning bathed in sun streaming in through the curtainless, east-facing window of my room. I felt rested although uncomfortable. They had rigged up a cage across my legs to keep the weight of the blankets off my wounded thighs. My left arm was bandaged and strapped to my side.

My immediate reaction was a desire to get up and out of here, but as soon as I tried to move my legs or arm I changed my mind. That wasn't going to be possible. The painkillers had worn off and any movement was excruciating agony. I gave in and accepted that I wasn't going to be playing golf for a few days yet.

Breakfast was brought in to me by a cheerful nurse who helped me butter my toast as I only had one arm operational. I munched my way through three slices of toast and marmalade (I'd asked for an extra one!) and I reflected back on the previous evening's events. I'd been damned lucky. Keith McDowell was a ruthless bastard. I had suspected that but I hadn't realised how much of an issue I had created for him. I was convinced that he would have had no compunction in getting rid of me permanently. Gavin Reid was clearly round the bend. There's probably some crazy title for his condition – post-adolescent mental pyromania disorder or some such cock-eyed term. As far as I was concerned he was just plain nuts and needed to be locked up. And I'm quite sure that anyone who had gone through what I had would agree with me.

With my hunger suitably satisfied I made myself as comfortable as I could, moving my limbs very gently, and tried to snooze.

I assumed that Bob Davis or one of his men would be round to visit to get my version of yesterday's events but, in fact, my first visitor was Pierre. He had got my message at the hotel and he came round mid-morning.

I was delighted to see him. I had been wondering how he had managed his Seventh Cavalry stunt and I was desperate to ask him. He enquired after my well-being. I assured him that I was OK and that according to the doctor I would be out in a few days and my wounds would be healed up.

I now felt sufficiently safe to be able to unburden myself. So first I explained to Pierre how I had suspected what had been going on.

"It was weird. If you remember we had worked our way

back to the lawyer, Reid, and the only person I knew who knew him was Keith McDowell. That in itself didn't help me much, but suddenly I remembered the article I had read about the death of Dewar in the mountains. You probably didn't notice it but it mentioned that he had been chairman of the Committee for Urban Planning. It was that that got me wondering. So I called my journalist friend in Edinburgh who did a little digging for me. He managed to find out that McDowell's Group is sitting on about twenty plots of land around the country which, if he could get planning permission for building more of his bloody supermarkets, would be worth a fortune to him. That got me wondering if he had been feeding money to Dewar through Reid and Purdy's crooked scheme at AIM in order to get planning permission pushed through more quickly. You know how difficult it is to get these things approved nowadays.

"It made some kind of sense. When we blew the AIM thing apart and Purdy disappeared he couldn't bribe Dewar any longer and keep far enough in the background to be safe. He could have tried to set up some other way of channelling money to Dewar but that would have been difficult without creating a fairly direct line between them. He must have decided to cut his losses and get rid of any chance that anyone could trace anything back to him. So he got Gavin Reid and his henchmen to eliminate me and Dewar."

"Why didn't you tell us?" asked Pierre.

"It seemed a bit far fetched at first. I wanted to find out more. I was going to tell you when I was sure. That's why I invited McDowell for that game of golf. I thought I might be able to steer the conversation a bit and confirm my theory. One big mistake. He must have already decided that he needed me out of the way. But he also needed to be sure that I hadn't spoken to anyone else. He wanted to know how much I knew or had guessed. Which explains all this."

"What the hell did they do to you?"

I explained briefly what had happened in that room and Pierre was very concerned and apologetic that they hadn't got there in time.

"I presume your three helpers were Mike, Doug and Mac? But how did you know where I was?"

He then told me how he had been worried the last time he had seen me and when I hadn't explained to him my thoughts he had had a chat with Mike. They had decided to put Mac and Doug on my tail for a few days just in case I was in any danger.

"They saw the kidnapping at the golf course but hadn't been able to do anything about it. Doug followed the car and Mac got in touch with Mike and me. When Doug saw you tied to the chair in that front room he sounded the alarm. We got organized as soon as we could but, unfortunately, not fast enough to save you from all this. I'm sorry."

"You don't need to be. I'll recover and there's no way any of these guys are going to wriggle out now. Kidnapping is one thing but kidnapping and torture is another. Bob Davis, the policeman, will make sure they go down for a very long time.

"Look Pierre, you'd better clear off now. I'm pretty sure the police will be round sometime today to take a statement from me and you'd better not be around when they come. I told them I had no idea who rescued me and I'll stick to that. I don't see any way they could guess. In fact they probably won't want to. I'll call you when they let me out and we'll fill in all the other bits then."

Pierre left, promising to thank the lads from me and to tell them I was more or less OK.

Bob Davis sent a sergeant round to take my statement

in the early afternoon. I explained to him the bare facts – my kidnapping, a reasonably detailed account of Reid's torturing, the arrival of Keith McDowell, the presence of Firkin and MacLean. I kept to the facts. I told him that there was no way I could identify my rescuers as they had been masked. I also told the sergeant that I would explain to his Inspector what the reasons were for the whole thing but I would prefer to wait a couple of days until I was more fully recovered.

"That's alright, sir," he said "This should be enough for us to be able to keep them in custody for the meantime. Inspector Davis asked me to tell you that he wished you a speedy recovery. The hospital told us that you would probably be allowed out the day after tomorrow."

"Thanks, officer. Just tell Inspector Davis from me a couple of things which are not in my statement – that the death of the SMP Bill Dewar in the mountains is related to this whole business and it was not an accident. It was deliberate murder. It was ordered by Keith McDowell and carried out by Firkin and MacLean via Gavin Reid. If he puts a bit of pressure on them I think one of them will confess. As soon as I'm mobile I'll come in and tell him all I know."

The sergeant left. I was, I admit, a bit tired after my two visitors and looked forward to a quiet afternoon's rest. The nurse gave me some more painkillers with my lunch and I was able to settle down for a relaxed snooze. I had a visit from the doctor who examined my wounds and assured me that, if I wanted to, I could probably leave the next day. There was no infection which was the thing he had been most concerned about.

I was woken up an hour or two later by a knock on the door and my friendly nurse popped her head round as she opened it.

"Got another visitor for you, Mr Bruce."

I wondered who this might be and tried to struggle up into a sitting position.

My first reaction was complete surprise but it was followed instantly by the realisation that this was just the visitor I wanted. She came a little tentatively into the room, her mouth shaped in a nervous smile and her eyes wide open with concern.

She made the few short steps across to my bed and took the outstretched hand that I raised to greet her.

"Lie still, Bob. You don't need to move."

She sat down on the chair beside my bed, still holding my hand. "I came as soon as I heard. What's happened to you? Are you going to be alright?"

Her eyes took in my strapped up arm and the cage across my thighs.

I was still so surprised that I hardly heard and didn't answer her questions straight away.

"How did you get here? Who told you where I was?"

Maggie relaxed when she heard my voice.

"Don't worry about that just now. I'm here – if that's alright with you."

"More than alright," I answered with genuine feeling. "I can't think of anyone I'd rather see. But how did you find out?"

"Your sister, Heather, phoned me as soon as she heard. She told me that you had been hurt and, if I wanted to see you, I should speak to a Pierre Collard at Fernie Castle Hotel and he would explain everything. So I just closed up the hotel and came as soon as I could."

"But why did Heather …?"

"I met Heather, if you remember, when she came to pick you up the last time you got yourself in a mess. She guessed that I would want to know and she guessed also that you would probably be fairly happy to see me. Was she right?"

I smiled at her. "She's too bloody smart, that woman."

"The doctor told me that you can get out tomorrow so, if you like, I'll come and take you home."

"And look after me like you did the last time?"

"Maybe," she replied mischievously. "Depends on how these wounds of yours are."

"They'll heal," I said.

"Yes, they'll heal."

Epilogue

Inspector Davis came round to see me the next morning rather than me having to travel into Cupar.

He had read about the resignation of Purdy from AIM but the real reason behind it had never been made public. Relying on his discretion I told him the whole story. I also explained that I had been to see the new management and made them aware of what had been going on. He considered that not to be any of his business and I promised I would let him know what they decided to do about the redistribution of the trust fund. He didn't ask me for any details about the "meeting" with Purdy which had led to his resignation.

I also explained how Keith McDowell had confirmed my suspicions about his use of AIM as a conduit for paying off Dewar for his work in helping to push planning permission through on the various supermarket projects he had stacked up.

I told him only what was relevant to his enquiries. He had evidence and proof of what he had found at McDowell's house although he admitted that he had no idea who had called him to warn him to get round there as fast as possible.

"I suppose I'll just have to put that one down to 'an anonymous tip off'," he said. "But how can I nail McDowell for Dewar's murder if you're sure that's what it was?"

"He admitted it to me – and in front of the three others who actually carried it out. My guess is they took him and dumped him using McDowell's helicopter. If you announce to the other three that you know maybe you can get them to turn Queen's evidence and be a witness for you."

He thought that was a tactic worth trying and thanked me for my help. I promised to be available for him if he needed anything else.

"I suppose you won't tell me who your three rescuers were?" he asked, on leaving.

"Sorry, I can't. I couldn't recognize them – perhaps they were buddies of the anonymous telephone caller. Anyway, they did do you a service, didn't they?" I said.

He looked at me closely "I'm bloody sure you do know, but I don't suppose I'll ever get it out of you – and, as you say, they did do me a service. I don't suppose they are a danger to the general public."

Ian McLeish called me to inform me that the Board of AIM had decided to be open about all of Purdy's misdeeds and that they would announce a wrapping up of the company and a distribution of an exceptional dividend to all the investors in addition to the net value that they realised.

He agreed to give an exclusive interview to Steven who, when I told him, was delighted.

The arrest of McDowell and the others was made public a few days later. A liquidator was appointed to manage his Group's business when it became clear that it was in a perilous financial position.

Firkin turned prosecution witness in exchange for a slightly reduced sentence. Keith McDowell was found guilty on two accounts of attempted murder and was locked away for a considerable time and Gavin Reid pleaded insanity and was committed to a mental institution for an indeterminate period.

As for APA Consulting – it still exists. We had a board meeting a couple of weeks later at the farm with Heather, Oliver and the rest of the family which now included Sophie and Maggie, as well as our new half-brother Pierre.